HOMETOWN HEARTS

SHIPMENT 1

Stranger in Town by Brenda Novak
Baby's First Homecoming by Cathy McDavid
Her Surprise Hero by Abby Gaines
A Mother's Homecoming by Tanya Michaels
A Firefighter in the Family by Trish Milburn
Tempted by a Texan by Mindy Neff

SHIPMENT 2

It Takes a Family by Victoria Pade
The Sheriff of Heartbreak County by Kathleen Creighton
A Hometown Boy by Janice Kay Johnson
The Renegade Cowboy Returns by Tina Leonard
Unexpected Bride by Lisa Childs
Accidental Hero by Loralee Lillibridge

SHIPMENT 3

An Unlikely Mommy by Tanya Michaels
Single Dad Sheriff by Lisa Childs
In Protective Custody by Beth Cornelison
Cowboy to the Rescue by Trish Milburn
The Ranch She Left Behind by Kathleen O'Brien
Most Wanted Woman by Maggie Price
A Weaver Wedding by Allison Leigh

SHIPMENT 4

A Better Ma
Daddy Protector
The Road to Bay
Fully Engaged
The Cowboy's Sec
A Husband's Wat

SHIPMENT 5

His Best Friend's Baby by Molly O'Keefe
Caleb's Bride by Wendy Warren
Her Sister's Secret Life by Pamela Toth
Lori's Little Secret by Christine Rimmer
High-Stakes Bride by Fiona Brand
Hometown Honey by Kara Lennox

SHIPMENT 6

Reining in the Rancher by Karen Templeton
A Man to Rely On by Cindi Myers
Your Ranch or Mine? by Cindy Kirk
Mother in Training by Marie Ferrarella
A Baby for the Bachelor by Victoria Pade
The One She Left Behind by Kristi Gold
Her Son's Hero by Vicki Essex

SHIPMENT 7

Once and Again by Brenda Harlen
Her Sister's Fiance by Teresa Hill
Family at Stake by Molly O'Keefe
Adding Up to Marriage by Karen Templeton
Bachelor Dad by Roxann Delaney
It's That Time of Year by Christine Wenger

SHIPMENT 8

The Rancher's Christmas Princess by Christine Rimmer
Their Baby Miracle by Lillian Darcy
Mad About Max by Penny McCusker
No Ordinary Joe by Michelle Celmer
The Soldier's Baby Bargain by Beth Kery
A Texan Under the Mistletoe by Leah Vale

HOMETOWN HEARTS

Her Surprise Hero

ABBY GAINES

HARLEQUIN® HOMETOWN HEARTS

ISBN-13: 978-0-373-21453-2

Her Surprise Hero

This edition published by arrangement with Harlequin Books S.A.

For questions and comments about the quality of this book, please contact us at CustomerService@Harlequin.com.

Printed in U.S.A.

Abby Gaines wrote for five years before she sold her first novel to Harlequin Superromance. During that time she worked as a business journalist and as an editor of a speedway magazine. Little wonder she has also contributed to the Harlequin NASCAR program.

Abby lives with her husband and children in a house with a sun-filled office whose sea view provides inspiration for the funny, romantic stories she loves to write. When she's not plotting her next book, Abby likes to read, travel and cook for friends. Visit her at abbygaines.com for details on upcoming books and more!

For Jasper, Imogen and Zoë.

You're the best.

With all my love, always.

Chapter One

"I'm not crazy." Cynthia Merritt crossed her fingers behind her back, in case that was a lie.

She fixed her gaze above her father's head, on the framed Harvard diplomas decorating the wall of his study. Her law degree and his, side by side.

"Of course you're not," Jonah Merritt soothed her, in a tone that would convince any jury of an insanity plea. "You're tired, that's all. Stressed."

Stressed. Cynthia could imagine how pathetic that sounded to her dad. Jonah Merritt had never once, in his illustrious legal career, succumbed to stress. And Cynthia had always been as stoic as her dad. She hated how disappointed he must be.

"It was just one incident," she promised. Funny how in her office or in the courtroom, she could be as cool as a defendant with a cast-iron alibi. But sitting in the wing chair in front of her father's desk, she was reduced to knotting her fingers in her lap.

"The problem is," Jonah said, "unless we act immediately, news of that *incident* will get around."

Everyone will hear the acting Georgia attorney general was found gibbering in a broom closet. Cynthia's face burned, unrelieved by the evening breeze wafting through the open sash window. "Dad, let me explain."

Her father held up a hand. "Let's look forward, not back, Cynthia. Everyone suffers the occasional glitch. Given your meteoric rise, it's hardly surprising you're not immune to the same stresses…my dear."

The tacked-on endearment surprised her and, though it was scarcely effusive, warmed her. She lowered her defenses long enough to smile. Her father lavished endearments on her youngest sister, Sabrina, and was affectionate with Megan, the middle Merritt girl. But he wasn't prone to showing affection toward

Cynthia. She'd always known she had his respect. But just sometimes, she yearned to see love, rather than pride, in his gaze.

Cynthia drew a breath that was unfortunately shuddery; she caught the scent of polished wood and leather that always made her think of her dad. "How do you suggest we progress from here?"

Jonah leaned forward, pleased with the question. "You need a break."

"A vacation?" she said. "Dad, I wouldn't know what to do with myself." *I wouldn't have anyone to go with.*

Her father chuckled. Back in the days before the heart attack that forced his retirement, his response to a suggested vacation would have mirrored hers. "Nothing as drastic as that. We'll get you out of town, but we'll make it look like a step forward in your career. People will assume the gossip can't be true."

A lump of lead settled in Cynthia's stomach, weighing her down in the chair. After yesterday's fiasco she should be thrilled her dad was still committed to supporting her career. But she was so tired, she almost wished he *was* sending her to the Caribbean, with or without company. "Great," she managed to say.

"I've talked to a few people." With Jonah's unrivaled connections in the Atlanta legal fraternity, that had to be an understatement. "Turns out they're looking for a state court judge down in Stonewall Hollow."

"I've never heard of it—and I thought we agreed I'm not ready to be a judge."

Her dad ran a hand through his hair impatiently. It was almost completely gray now, a reminder he wasn't as strong physically as he'd been a year ago. "Stonewall Hollow is a small town a couple of hours south. They're offering a temporary position—the present judge is on extended leave for health reasons. You're not ready for the Atlanta judiciary, Cynthia, but this is exactly the kind of experience that will get you ready."

"How—how temporary?" She was being *banished.* She wedged her fingers beneath her thighs, against the seat cushion.

"A couple of months." Jonah relaxed as far as his high-backed leather chair allowed. "You'll cut your teeth in a place where not much happens, then come back to Atlanta with a new dimension of experience that will serve you, and the city, well."

It was three years since some of her dad's colleagues had first suggested Cynthia Merritt had what it took to make judge. A couple of her father's pals on the superior court had even said she was potential Georgia Supreme Court material. The supreme court!

Jonah had passed their comments on to Cynthia casually, but he'd been thrilled. So had she. Together, they'd made the decision to broaden her experience, and she'd left Merritt, Merritt & Finch, the family law firm, to work as a district attorney. A welcome banishment, that one. Her elevation to interim state attorney general following the sudden death of the incumbent had been a real coup.

Shame about the broom closet.

"Your career has moved so fast, it's no wonder the pressure grew too much," her father ruminated, evidently thinking along the same lines. "A change of pace will be just the thing."

"Dad, do I have to go away?" Couldn't she just curl up in her father's lap, the way she used to when she was five years old, before Sabrina was born? *Of course not.* But at least here in Atlanta, she knew exactly where she fit, even if lately the fit hadn't felt right.

"It will be difficult for you to continue in the attorney general role after yesterday." Jonah rolled his gold-plated fountain pen between his fingers. "More than difficult. Jake won't allow it."

Jake Warrington, Sabrina's husband, was the governor of Georgia. He'd been reluctant to accept his staff's recommendation to appoint his sister-in-law in the acting role, worried about accusations of nepotism. Though he'd eventually been persuaded, he'd made it clear that at the first whiff Cynthia wasn't up to the job, she'd be out.

No way could he ignore the stench of the broom closet.

Cynthia scooted to the edge of her seat. "I could go back to the D.A.'s office." One last stand against the inevitable sentence.

"Your colleagues on the other side of the courtroom will take every opportunity to undermine your credibility," her father pointed out.

She'd do the same to any lawyer foolish enough to crack under pressure.

"Let's be honest, Cynthia," Jonah said. "Your future is decidedly shaky."

Normally, she was a big fan of honesty, to the extent she could be too blunt. She got that from her dad. So it was stupid to sit here wishing he'd just said, *I don't care what you did. You're my daughter and I love you.*

"Better to leave town, get through this, and come back with judging credentials no one can ignore." Her dad wasn't giving her a choice. "You should see a doctor before you leave, have him give you something to calm your nerves."

"I won't take it," Cynthia said automatically. Her father nodded. The Merritts drew on inner strength, not drugs. She thought about not seeing her dad, or her sisters, for two months, and rubbed her arms.

"What is it, Cynthia?" he asked gently.

"I just want to get past this," she said. "I want to get back to how things were."

Impossible. Because her meltdown hadn't been triggered purely by work stresses, no matter what her father thought.

In the past year, her two sisters had fallen in love with men who adored them. Cynthia had always been out in front of Megan and Sabrina: she set the pace, they struggled to keep up. Now, they'd been admitted to some exclusive, blissful club, and she could only stand outside, nose pressed to the window, envying them.

Unconsciously, she touched her nose. They would be shocked, maybe even disappointed, to hear about her fall from grace. Megan had called Cynthia's cell yesterday, but Cynthia hadn't picked up. Which was crazy—*that word again*—because her sisters loved her, they were her best friends. "Dad, please, let me stay in Atlanta."

In court, Jonah could mold the toughest witness like putty…but a disintegrating daughter was beyond his capacity. After a moment's hesitation, he walked around the mahogany desk to pat her shoulder. "Cynthia, sweetheart, this is for the best."

Sweetheart? He really did think she was nuts. Fleetingly, Cynthia yearned for the broom closet at the attorney general's office on Capitol Square. The coziness of the dark confines, the musty, dusty smell that intimated the undisturbed passing of time…

She was losing what was left of her mind. And since her mind was by far her biggest asset—she didn't have Sabrina's beauty or Megan's sweet nature—she snapped to attention and clamped her hands over the arms of her chair.

"I'll do it," she said. "I'll go to Stonewall Hollow."

The Griffin County Courthouse sat smack in the middle of downtown Stonewall Hollow.

The redbrick building's colonnaded facade was disproportionate to its size, as if some nineteenth-century architect had overreached his brief in the quest for professional glory.

"You and me both," Cynthia murmured to the nameless, long-deceased architect as she gazed up at the building from the bottom of the marble steps. She'd been so obsessed with being appointed the youngest-ever judge in the Georgia Supreme Court, she'd gone beyond her capabilities in accepting the interim attorney general role.

Her confidence, which had grown with every mile she'd put between herself and Atlanta, wavered. She was the new girl on her first day in town. Not just the new girl, the new *judge.* No room for nerves if she wanted to do her job properly. She switched her briefcase from her right hand to her left, testing its reassuring weight. Then she buttoned her suit jacket and walked up the steps.

The huge, wooden double doors stood open, admitting the Monday morning sunlight to the marble-floored foyer. Inside, more pillars supported a mezzanine that revealed a view of a domed ceiling three stories up, painted with a frieze of classical gods and goddesses riding on pink-tinged clouds. They really had gone overboard with this place.

This *empty* place. It struck Cynthia there was no security screening, as there was at Fulton County Court in Atlanta. And no clusters of lawyers and their clients. *Because there's no judge,* she reminded herself. *Until now.*

To her right, a small sign promising Information was almost obscured by a poster advertising the county fair, coming up on the Fourth of July weekend. Next to the poster was a counter with a window.

Cynthia rang the bell on the counter—a real bell, the old-fashioned kind, rather than a buzzer.

"Just one moment," a woman called. A couple of dozen moments passed before she appeared. Dark hair sprinkled with gray and a curvy shape that had spread in all directions suggested she was in her fifties, but she moved at the deliberate pace of someone older. "Can I help you?" She spoke slowly, too.

"I'm Cynthia Merritt."

"The new judge?" *Judge* became two syllables. The woman looked at her askance. "It's nine o'clock in the morning."

"I know I'm a little late, but—"

"Oh, honey—I mean, Your Honor." The woman chortled. "We weren't expecting you until midday, is all. You must have left Atlanta in the middle of the night."

Cynthia had been on the road at six-thirty, the usual time she left her apartment to go to work.

The older woman stuck a hand through the information window. "I'm Melanie Wilkes. Yes—" she laughed, delighted at Cynthia's double take "—just like in *Gone with the Wind.* I think my mama was gone with the whiskey when she named me..." She paused; this was clearly a well-worn joke. Cynthia smiled through her nerves.

"I'm your secretary—I'm just filling in on the information desk until Faye-Anne arrives. But I'm going to close this window right now and take you upstairs." Melanie appeared in the foyer a minute later. At the top of the sweeping staircase, she paused to take several deep breaths. "You do look very young, Your Honor."

From what Cynthia had seen of the quiet town, she doubted the local crime rate would tax her abilities, no matter how little experience she had. "I'm older than I look." Should she admit to thirty-two? Or hope the woman would assume thirty-five plus?

"And you're a lady."

"Uh, yes." Pressure built behind Cynthia's temples, and she took a slow breath.

"There's folks around here can't abide the thought of a lady judge," Melanie warned. "I'm not one of them, let me tell you that."

"Pleased to hear it," Cynthia said coolly.

Melanie beamed. "Oh, yes, that's very good, Your Honor. You use that voice and everyone will know who's boss."

Should Cynthia tell the woman to stop calling her Your Honor? Enough with the uncertainty. "How about you call me Cynthia when it's just the two of us," she told Melanie. "And Judge Merritt in public." She was determined to fit in with the less formal atmosphere of a small-town courthouse.

"Yes, ma'am." Melanie saluted sloppily. "Let me show you your chambers." She crossed the spacious second-floor reception area and opened an oak-paneled door that made Cynthia think of her father.

Sunlight streamed into the large, airy space, dazzling her for a moment. A leather-topped oak desk sat between two sash windows, flanked by two flags—the Stars and Stripes to the left, and on the right, the Stars and Bars of Georgia.

In front of the desk were a pair of serviceable chairs. Cynthia tried to imagine hearing lawyers' arguments from the other side, from the cracked maroon leather seat that looked as if it had been there a couple of decades before she was born. It seemed absurd that she could go from lawyer to judge in the space of Friday's brief swearing-in ceremony and this morning's three-hour drive. But although, in theory, all Georgia judges were elected to their positions, in reality most were like her—lawyers appointed to a judge position between elections. When the election came around they competed to retain their seat. Which she would not be doing in Stonewall Hollow.

"This carpet is…unusual." Cynthia stepped back to gain a better perspective. The enormous rug covered almost the entire room. It depicted a Civil War battle scene, Confederate soldiers bayoneting their Union opponents.

"Battle of Kennesaw Mountain, woven by the Daughters of the American Revolution," Melanie informed her proudly. "There's a little bit of my great-great-grandmother in there. Not literally, of course."

"It must be valuable," Cynthia said. "Wouldn't it be better off in a museum?" She didn't relish seeing the bloodthirsty scene every time she crossed the room.

"The museum's full up and the rug's always been right here on this floor," Melanie told her. "We value our traditions here in Stonewall Hollow. Now, you have your own bathroom." She pointed to a door in the far corner. "Judge Cartwright had it installed after he—" she lowered her voice to a loud whisper "—lost control of his bladder. That was three judges ago," she added hastily, seeing Cynthia's alarm.

Anxious to move on from judicial incontinence, Cynthia pointed to another oak-paneled door, adjacent to the bathroom. "What's in there?"

"That's just a broom closet."

Cynthia's head snapped around. Had they heard? Could they possibly know?

Melanie met her shocked expression with a look of polite inquiry.

Of course they don't know.

"It seems an odd location for a broom closet," Cynthia explained.

"I don't think there are any actual brooms

in there these days," Melanie said. "The janitor keeps all of that stuff down in the basement." She crossed the room, opened the door. "Nope, just a couple of file boxes." She smiled brightly at Cynthia. "Now, how about I make you a coffee?"

"Coffee sounds great." Turning resolutely away from the closet, Cynthia made for the desk and sat down. The leather creaked, but its wornness made it comfortable. She noticed a small bronze statue of Lady Justice on the mantelpiece. The blindfolded, toga-clad woman held the traditional sword and set of scales. She was a symbol of blind justice, or as the inscription on the United States Supreme Court building in Washington, D.C., put it: Equal justice under law.

That was what Cynthia needed, a fair shot at recovering from what her dad called a "glitch," at getting back to her life as soon as possible.

Melanie returned with the coffee. "The mayor will be in to see you around lunchtime—he wasn't expecting you so early."

Cynthia listened while her assistant outlined the other visitors she might expect today. "And I daresay Ethan Granger will pop in," Melanie finished.

"Who's he?"

But Melanie was now running through a list of courthouse staff that Cynthia would never remember. She did manage to latch on to the name of the clerk of the court, Jim Hopkins.

"When can we expect the attorneys to resume cases?" she asked when Melanie paused for breath.

"The ones that were underway before Judge Piet took sick, those guys should be ready to go," Melanie said. "The new ones, we need to start issuing court dates. It'll be crazy around here for a while."

"How big is the backlog?" Cynthia had imagined a state judge in one of Georgia's least populated counties would deal with the occasional overnight arrest and spend the rest of her time sentencing traffic offences and hearing civil disputes.

"Maybe a couple hundred cases," Melanie said. "But there'll be more, don't you worry. Summer is our busy season—all those kids out of school and back from college, with nothing to do but hunt trouble. I tell you, by the time September rolls around, the Sheriff is ready to check himself into a nut farm."

The walls of the spacious chambers began

to close in on Cynthia. "Fine," she said thinly, envisaging herself working all hours to stay on top of Stonewall Hollow's crime wave. So much for de-stressing.

At her request, Melanie brought in the transcripts of the most recent hearings, along with the cases that had been on the docket right before the former judge took ill. There was also a stack of restraining order petitions, ex parte orders and various other petitions that required more information before Cynthia could make much sense of them.

She got down to work. Her assistant was right, the town was in the middle of a mini crime wave. The docket was five single-spaced pages. Even allowing for the usual no-shows and continuances, she couldn't imagine how her predecessor had hoped to get through so many cases in one day. And these were only the misdemeanors—traffic violations, property offences and simple assaults. Felony cases were heard in the superior court in the next county.

Melanie had said a lot of the defendants would be young people, college kids. Cynthia had spent her college years in the Harvard library; she'd never been in on student pranks. Now, she had to pass judgment on people whose age she'd been not so long ago. And on older people, whose experiences, again, she hadn't shared. In the past, she'd have assumed she could make the transition with ease, but right now, nothing felt certain.

She drank three cups of coffee, belatedly aware her veins were buzzing. The courthouse clock struck noon, and she took the chime as a cue to push away the transcript she was reading and kick back in her chair.

Before she could relax, she heard her door creak open. A trim, middle-aged man entered, hand outstretched. "Judge Merritt, welcome to Stonewall Hollow. I'm Mayor Larsen. Richard Larsen."

"Please, call me Cynthia." She shook his hand.

He took a seat uninvited, rubbing his palms together like a boy scout trying to start a fire. "Well, well, a lady judge, right here in Stonewall Hollow."

He might have been saying, "An alien invasion, right here in Stonewall Hollow."

Didn't this town have television?

"Move over, Judge Judy." The mayor answered her unspoken question. "*We* have Judge Cynthia."

She wasn't sure what was worse: people

doubting her competence because she was a woman, or expecting her to become a pop culture icon of justice. "I'm afraid my courtroom won't be of much entertainment value."

The mayor's face fell, but he said, "Of course not. Sheriff Davis will stop by later, fill you in on things. I know he's hoping the courthouse will be open for business again by next week."

"We'll be open for business tomorrow," Cynthia said. They'd need to be, with that backlog.

Mayor Larsen blinked. "Uh...excellent. Some big-city efficiency coming to town." He chuckled. "When folk get word of it, you'll have a few people bending your ear. Everyone's got something to say about the way this place works."

Cynthia wasn't sure what he meant. A small town might be less formal, but surely the place worked in accordance with the Georgia legal system? She let it go, offered a few platitudes about how she was looking forward to working with the locals.

"You'll want to come down hard on shoplifters." The mayor cracked his knuckles. "Morale is always better when we're tough on crime that affects small business owners."

Store owners' morale wasn't her responsibility. "I'll judge appropriately" was all the commitment she would make.

"Excellent." He beamed his approval as he said his goodbyes.

The moment he left, Cynthia extended her arms out in front of her, spreading her fingers wide to stretch her stiff muscles.

Mayor Larsen's head popped back around the door; she whipped her hands down.

"You'll need to talk to Ethan Granger," he said. And was gone.

After the mayor, she had a visit from the clerk of the court. "Ask me anything about the docket," Jim Hopkins challenged her, white teeth gleaming against his dark face. "See if I don't know the answer."

She dredged up a couple of questions, which he answered rapid-fire.

Then came a social worker from Albany who'd been assigned a handful of cases in Stonewall Hollow, and the sheriff. Each visitor barged in, her only warning the squeak of unoiled hinges. What counted for discourtesy in Atlanta must be a local custom in Stonewall Hollow. They all wanted to tell her "how we do things around here." All three mentioned the importance of talking to Ethan Granger.

"Who's he?" Cynthia asked each time. She

received three wildly varying answers. Ethan Granger was a saint, a one-man rehabilitation service, or wasting his time on a kid who'd never amount to anything.

That last view was the sheriff's. He clapped his hat to his chest and announced, "I like Ethan, make no mistake, everyone does. But this time he's bitten off more'n he can chew."

Him and me both.

The sheriff explained how his department worked—flat out, all the time—and the names of the D.A.s. Cynthia propped her chin in her palm and tried to focus. When he shared the good news that Cynthia's court would hear an overflow of cases from a neighboring county, she was tempted to jump into her Volvo and hightail it back to Atlanta.

As the sheriff left, with as little ceremony as he'd arrived, steel bands of pressure tightened around her forehead and wrists. Maybe she should have taken those pills her doctor had prescribed. They were in the glove compartment of her car, she could duck outside and…

No. She was cut from the same cloth as her father, and Jonah Merritt would never do that. Even after his cardiac surgery, he'd restricted his meds to the minimum. He liked to keep his mind clear, and would want her to do the same.

Dad's not here.

She'd spent her life living up to her father's expectations and she wasn't about to drop her standards now that a few hundred miles lay between them. Besides, he had a knack for finding out things. When Cynthia was eight years old, she'd taken the credit for a painting her father had admired on the classroom wall. Somehow, her dad had discovered it was her friend's handiwork. His disappointment had been far more painful than the swat he'd dealt to Cynthia's backside.

She lifted her fifth—or was it her sixth?—cup of coffee to her lips and noticed her hand was shaking. Not to mention her heart was pounding like a gavel in a courtroom riot. Cynthia clattered the cup down onto the desk; coffee slopped over the side.

"Blast." As she pulled a tissue from her purse, her elbow connected with the cup, knocking it off the desk.

"Dammit." Cynthia jumped to her feet as coffee spilled across the Civil War carpet. Her first day on the job and she'd ruined a priceless rug. "Don't move," she warned the spreading stain, then jogged to the bathroom.

She returned with a fistful of paper towels and spread them over the mess. The coffee seeped through the paper.

She needed a sponge. Melanie would know where to find one…yikes…what if the coffee had obliterated Melanie's great-great-grandmother's handiwork?

Cynthia's eyes strayed to the broom closet.

No sponges in there. No brooms, either.

Just a cool, dark, quiet space where no one would tell her how to do her job or alarm her with stories of ratcheting crime rates….

Cynthia snapped her gaze away from the door, unable to believe she was seriously tempted to hide in another broom closet.

On the other hand, maybe there was a sponge in there Melanie didn't know about….

She took three steps before she came to her senses. *Stay away from the closet.*

Out in the reception, she heard a shrill female voice. "A lady judge? What in the world will happen next?" As if the end of civilization was right around the corner, and Cynthia was personally responsible. "Has Ethan been in yet?" the unknown woman asked.

Cynthia's head throbbed. It was so bright in these south-facing chambers. The sun hadn't let up all day and the air conditioner was distinctly underpowered. If she could find some shade…she eyed the closet.

"I'm looking for a sponge," she said out loud. "That's all."

She pulled the door open. As Melanie had said, the space held two file cartons. On the left-hand side was a stack of deep shelves. There could be an old sponge somewhere in there, she reasoned. She stepped inside. The dimness immediately eased her headache. Before she could think about it, she pulled the door closed.

Blessed silence. Dust motes tickled her nose. Oh, yeah, she was definitely crazy…but right now, she didn't care. Cynthia reached through the darkness and patted the dusty shelves. Her fingers traveled all the way into the corners. No cleaning materials. She sat on the stacked file boxes and took a calming breath. There, that was better. But if she stayed in here another second, she'd be repeating history. She shook out her fingers to loosen the tension.

As she reached for the door handle, she heard the sound that had driven her crazy all afternoon. The creak of the door to her chambers. A man said, "Judge Merritt?"

Cynthia froze. *Go away.*

"She's not here." He raised his voice, presumably calling to Melanie.

That's right, I'm not here. So, leave.

"Are you sure?" Great, now Melanie arrived. As soon as Cynthia got out of the closet, she was ordering a lock for the door. "She was at her desk a moment ago. I would have seen if she'd come out. Maybe she's in there."

For one awful moment, Cynthia imagined her assistant pointing at the closet. Then she realized Melanie must mean the bathroom. If they went to check, Cynthia could slip out...

"I can stop by later." The man's voice was deep and slow.

Great idea, Cynthia encouraged him.

"Oh, dear." Melanie sounded as if she was moving away. "The judge must have spilled her coffee. I'll go find a cloth."

The door squeaked as Melanie left. Had the man gone, too? Cynthia held her breath, listening.

The dust motes chose that moment to turn hostile. She scrunched her face in the effort to control her sinuses. But it was no good.

Cynthia sneezed.

Chapter Two

Thankfully, it wasn't a proper sneeze, more a teeny explosion of breath. No one could have heard—

The closet door was wrenched open. Light flooded in.

"Well, hello." A man loomed in front of Cynthia. "Judge Merritt, I presume?" Puzzlement, laced with amusement, all wrapped up in a deliberate, country drawl.

Cynthia processed broad shoulders and a cowboy hat that he removed as she bustled forward. "I was trying to find a sponge to clean up the coffee I spilled."

"With the door shut."

Worn denim-blue T-shirt, faded jeans, work boots. Probably not a lawyer.

"It swung closed behind me," she said.

He glanced at the door and moved his hand toward it. If he dared test its swing, she'd find some way of sending him to jail for ten years. He met her narrowed eyes and dropped his hand.

"I heard you come in," she continued, "and I thought it would look odd if I came out of the broom closet. *Closet,*" she amended hastily. "It's just a closet, no brooms."

"And no sponge," he suggested.

She nodded once. His brown eyes wandered over her, making Cynthia want to squirm. She held herself rigid.

"You're right," he agreed, "it does look odd."

"Exactly why I didn't come out," she said sharply. She proffered a hand. "I'm Cynthia Merritt."

When her hand met his, she realized hers was dusty. That didn't stop him clasping it in a firm grip that made her palm tingle.

"Ethan Granger."

This was the man everyone wanted her to meet? She put aside her embarrassment and scrutinized him with equal frankness.

Cynthia was tall at five-nine, but Ethan had

several inches on her. His hair was the rich, dark brown of the tilled earth she'd seen as she drove through the remotest parts of Georgia; his gold-flecked irises managed to be both warm and intense at the same time. Rugged. That's how she'd describe his face, which held an entirely different kind of strength from her father's. His tan suggested he worked outdoors, and lines at the corners of his eyes told her he either laughed a lot or he squinted into the sun. She chose the latter—the firm set of his jaw said he took life seriously.

But even allowing for lax small-town standards, Ethan Granger didn't look like a social worker, a probation officer, or anyone involved in the judicial process.

"You have dust on your forehead." Ethan pulled a handkerchief from his pocket and held it out.

"Thank you, but I'm fine."

"Shall I do it?"

She grabbed the hanky from him and wiped her forehead.

"You missed some." Ethan took the handkerchief and dabbed at a spot above her left eye. For a big-handed, blunt-fingered guy, he had a gentle touch.

Goose bumps puckered her forearms, despite the powerful afternoon sunlight. Great, first she was in the broom closet, now she was having a sensual reaction to a stranger. She took a step back. "I'm sure it's fine now."

He gave her an unhurried smile; he was the best-looking man she'd met in a long time, no question. "You're welcome," he said.

Melanie trotted in, carrying a dripping towel. "I can't find the judge, but I brought this." She came to an abrupt stop. "Judge Merritt. There you are."

"The judge was looking for a sponge," Ethan said. Cynthia froze. "In the bathroom."

Cynthia let her shoulders relax. "Thanks for bringing that, Melanie, just what we need."

The woman knelt to wipe the rug. "I see you've met Ethan," she observed, with a kind of proprietary pride.

"The judge and I were just about to get down to business," Ethan said.

Cynthia bristled. Letting her off the hook about the closet didn't give him the right to call the shots.

"Lovely." Melanie glanced up from her sponging. "While I'm here, Judge, Mrs. Marks from the Stonewall Hollow Heritage Society came by to invite you to tomorrow night's potluck."

Mrs. Marks owned the shrill voice that had driven her into the closet, she guessed.

"Half the town's likely to be there," Melanie prompted her. She gripped the edge of the desk and used it to pull herself to her feet, with a huff of effort. "My sister and I always bring a ton of food, so you don't need to worry about cooking."

"Thanks, but I have a lot of reading to catch up on." Cynthia waved in the direction of her desk. "Could you pass on my apology?"

As Melanie left, Cynthia brushed her hands down her skirt, leaving a trail of dust. Ethan's glance followed the movement. Was he about to start wiping her skirt? She bolted for her chair.

The barrier provided by the enormous desk helped put things back on a proper footing. "What can I do for you, Mr. Granger?"

"Ethan," he corrected her as he proceeded to dwarf one of her visitor chairs. "You and I will likely get to know each other pretty well, we might as well start off right."

Since being found in a closet could in no way be considered starting off right, Cynthia didn't protest the first-name issue. She repeated, "What can I do for you?"

"It's more what I can do for you," he drawled.

No matter that the words were patently innocuous, they washed over her and left her...warm. She touched her left cheek to be sure she wasn't blushing. Of course she wasn't.

"I understand you're...some kind of social worker?" she asked.

One corner of his mouth lifted. "Nope, I'm not much good at touchy-feely jargon." He talked so slowly, it was like waiting for grass to grow. Yet intelligence gleamed in his eyes. "I own the Double T ranch," he said. "Most of the kids who get into trouble with the law in this town end up working for me."

"You employ them?" Cynthia picked up her silver pen and wrote *Ethan Granger* at the top of her legal pad. "That's admirable."

"They carry out their community service sentence at my place. I run a work program."

Community service, she wrote. "Presumably in parallel with counseling?"

He leaned back in his chair, long legs stretched out in front. "These kids mainly need some focus to keep them out of trouble. I provide that focus. Rather than formal counseling, I get alongside the guys, teach them skills that might come in handy when they're looking for work. Listen to them. They talk when they want to."

Cynthia wondered how effective those conversations were, with his distaste for "touchy-feely."

"Who supervises your program?" she asked, pen poised.

He clasped his hands behind his head, elbows wide. "I do."

"Are you qualified to work with convicted teenagers, Mr. Granger?" She jotted a couple of question marks after his name.

She sensed his silence was from his reining in his irritation, but it didn't show on his face.

"I know how these kids think," he said. "I had more than a few wild moments as a teen myself."

He'd have been taller than his friends, she guessed. A natural leader. But she couldn't imagine him being *wild.*

"You have no idea," he said.

"Excuse me?"

"I was fortunate to get back on the right track. Now I'm an upstanding citizen, like yourself." Those umber eyes were on her again. Judging her. "I'd bet a million bucks you never did anything wild in your life."

Judging was *her* job. Cynthia straightened in her chair. "How much does the county pay you to run your program, Mr. Granger? And how many hours' free labor do you get from these young people?"

He tensed, but didn't move from his laid-back position. "I'll have to check my records to give you the exact amount. But whatever *free labor* I get is chewed up by the time I put into the kids." There was an edge to the drawl.

Did he have something to hide? She wrote *Talk to Sheriff re program $$.*

Ethan dropped his laconic pose faster than she'd have guessed he could move. He shot to his feet and leaned over her desk, hands splayed on the surface. "I told you, I'll check my records," he said pleasantly.

"I'll let you know if that's necessary." She stood. "Thank you for coming in, Mr. Granger, it's been useful."

He straightened. "Ethan," he reminded her. "Judge Piet often talks to me about the kids before he sentences them, to work out if it's best to send them to me."

"That sounds most irregular."

"It works well. I'd like you to do the same." Still pleasant, but with a firmness that made it plain he was yet another person telling her how to do her job.

"You're not a social worker or probation officer or any other professional appropriate to that kind of discussion," she pointed out. "You're a civilian who benefits from community service hours." It was a gross conflict of interest.

"I'm a civilian who cares about kids who get into trouble."

"And I'm the judge who determines the sentence an offender should receive." She moved around the desk, indicating as clearly as she could it was time he left. "If I need your input, you can be sure I'll ask."

Ethan bit down on his frustration and counted to ten—a preventative technique that was second nature to him now. As always, he kept his face impassive, a match for his neutral tone. He hadn't lost his temper in nearly fifteen years, and he wasn't about to let the new judge provoke him. He eyed Cynthia's face, her sharp chin tilted up, and wondered how he could have thought, when he found her in the closet, that she looked soft.

Must have been the way the particles of dust had floated around her, blurring her prickly edges. Her wide gray eyes had helped, along with her full mouth, which had quivered before she slipped behind her professional mask.

"Do you have Ben Miller's case there?"

With a dip of his head, he indicated the docket on her desk.

"That's none of your business." She headed for the door.

"The boy needs a kick in the pants, a reminder that if he doesn't raise his game he won't make it to college," Ethan said. "He needs to understand that the alternative to an education isn't a lot of fun."

She grasped the door handle. "Next you'll be saying hard, physical work on your ranch is the cure," she suggested, saccharin-sweet.

"It is. I know that kid. Give him a few unoccupied hours and he'll find trouble. Keep him busy—"

Cynthia pulled the door open, and flung her other arm wide. "How about I do my job, Mr. Granger, and you do yours?"

"Your *job* being to suspect me of milking the system before you've known me two minutes?" He walked toward her, using his superior height to…not to intimidate, he hadn't done that in years. Just to let her know she didn't get to trample all over him in her shiny black high-heeled shoes. "You're here to serve this town. I'm trying to help you understand the needs of some of its people." Up close, he caught the scent of her perfume. Lilies, with something spicy.

"I'm here to mete out justice. Individual circumstances can be brought up for consideration at sentencing."

"This place doesn't run like any city courthouse."

"I know. People keep barging into my chambers uninvited," she said pointedly.

Her undertone of humor took him by surprise. Disarmed him.

Ethan looked down at her. She didn't seem hostile now. More...stressed. Had to be tough, first day in a new job, new town. He spread his hands in apology. "I'm sorry I barged in, but I wanted to talk to you before you start hearing cases. Not just about my work program, there's something else I need to say."

Cynthia sighed, but she closed the door and returned to the desk. Ethan settled into his chair, too. He quashed his reservations. This wasn't about his personal comfort level, this was his family. "Among those cases—" he jerked his thumb at the docket "—is Sam Barrett's. My son."

He wondered if he'd ever get used to saying *my son.*

She glanced at the pages. "I don't recall the details." Her cool tone told him to butt out.

But as Ethan was fast learning, where your kid's concerned, everything's your business. Futile to wish he'd been able to build up to the role of father slowly, starting with holding a helpless baby in his arms. Discovering he had an eighteen-year-old son, one who took after Ethan in all the worst ways, was a shock he was still grappling with, along with the slew of parenting techniques he was failing to acquire.

"He's up for vandalizing the library," he told Cynthia. "Graffiti."

Disapproval clouded her features.

Ethan leaned forward, hands clasped between his knees. "He's not a bad kid, he's just been hanging around with some unsuitable influences." He imagined every parent in history had told the authorities—and themselves—the same thing when their child got into trouble. "He's been through a difficult time. But he'll plead guilty…he's honest, at least."

"Mr. Granger, this information can be presented in court, presentencing. It's not appropriate—"

"I want you to sentence him to work for

me," Ethan blurted. He knew immediately he'd handled it wrong.

Cynthia's hands lifted from the desk as if he'd sent a thousand volts across the surface. "You're trying to dictate what sentence I should hand out to your son?"

"Sam's only been with me for three months." The back of Ethan's neck heated. "He's eighteen, he can leave whenever he likes, get into whatever trouble he can find. I'm already on borrowed time—I need to straighten him out fast."

"A process you have well under control."

Ethan's veins felt as if they were pushing blood faster than his thumping heart could handle; something was about to burst. He measured each word as he delivered it. "I can't help Sam if I'm not with him. If you sentence him to work with me, I'll be able to engage with him. He'll be *forced* to engage with me." And hopefully do more than grunt at Ethan. Unfortunately, he wouldn't put money on that.

"Mr. Granger, the court isn't your personal parenting support service." Two spots of color appeared in Cynthia's cheeks. "I resent being told how to do my job."

"I resent the look in my son's eyes that says he despises me," Ethan shot back. And realized what he'd said. He clamped his mouth shut. Dammit, he'd put resentment and bitterness—the foundations of the kind of anger that led a man to his breaking point—behind him. Yet the new judge had him more riled in five minutes than he'd been in over a decade. *It's this trouble with Sam.* He was walking on damned eggshells so much around the boy, not to mention struggling to listen to his own mother's "advice" on the subject without snapping, he was venting on the judge.

Cynthia folded her arms across her chest. Incongruously, Ethan noticed she was curvier than he might have expected for such a slim woman.

"Your conflict of interest is even more blatant than I thought," she said.

"Small town is a synonym for conflict of interest," he told her. "Everyone knows everybody else's business and doesn't hesitate to share an opinion. You need to understand that, get used to it."

"And you need to get used to my professionalism." Her shoulders were stiff as concrete; Ethan had the bizarre urge to run his fingers over them, to loosen her up.

"I know I can help Sam," he said. A lie. He'd never been less certain of anything. He'd never wanted anything so much. "I'm asking you to *mete out justice* in a way that gives me and my son a chance."

Her gaze wandered somewhere to Ethan's right. Following it, he saw a statue of Lady Justice on the mantelpiece. He levered himself out of his chair and went over to the statue. He weighed the cool bronze in his right hand. "Justice isn't always about the law."

"My professors at Harvard would beg to differ." She sounded distant, as if she was breathing the rarefied air of the Ivy League.

He needed her here, in the real world where his real son was causing him real problems. "I'm sure you can think of times when applying the law didn't serve the cause of justice." He caught a flicker in her eyes, and pressed his case. "I need you to do what's right for me and my son."

"I will do the right thing," Cynthia said. "You can rest assured of that."

An entirely unsatisfactory response. But if he argued, Ethan risked making a bad situation worse. He set Justice back in her place, watching over the judge. "Then I'll see you in Court."

"Fine."

It wasn't fine. She radiated hostility and he needed to fix that. Hostility tended to grow overnight, like mushrooms in fall. That wouldn't serve Sam tomorrow. He stuck out his hand, forcing her to make the neutral contact.

It turned out shaking hands with the judge in no way counted as neutral. Ethan couldn't help registering the softness of her fingers that belied the firmness of her grip, the intriguing smoke-gray eyes.

Maybe he should ask her to dinner so he could explain more about the work he did with teenagers.

No way. She'd turn him down faster than she could say "conflict of interest," and she might hold a dinner invitation against Sam tomorrow.

Judge Merritt may be the prettiest woman he'd met in a long time, but that was irrelevant.

Ethan would judge the Judge strictly on her performance in court.

Chapter Three

"All rise for the Honorable Judge Merritt presiding," the bailiff intoned. "Court is now in session."

Cynthia's heels tapped against the polished floorboards as she took her first steps into the courtroom as a judge. The sound echoed in the cavernous space, bouncing off the pressed steel ceiling high above. Sunlight filtered through the semisheer blinds that covered the tall windows. Though it was a bright day, low-hanging lamps supplemented the natural light. The frosted glass shades looked old enough to have been here since the electric lightbulb was invented.

She sat down at the bench which, unlike in a modern courtroom, wasn't raised above floor level. To her left was the witness stand and the six seats used by the jury in a state court jury trial—they were empty today. To her right, the dock where the defendants would stand. Two dark cherrywood tables for lawyers and their clients faced the bench. Immediately behind, a wooden rail separated the officials' area from the pew-style public seating.

And in the front pew stood Ethan Granger.

Cynthia adjusted her robe as everyone sat. She drew confidence from the authority the black garment imparted.

The public seating, street level and mezzanine, was surprisingly full given this morning's caseload: a few college kids charged with various misdemeanors, a DUI, a dad being sued for child support payments. And Sam Barrett.

She'd asked Melanie about Sam right after Ethan left her chambers. This wasn't the first time the boy had been in trouble, so she was able to read the transcripts of his previous trials. If he'd only been in Stonewall Hollow three months, he hadn't wasted any time finding the wrong side of the law.

Cynthia had a bad feeling about Sam and his dad; she'd lain awake last night in the cottage she'd rented sight unseen before she arrived. Around 3 a.m. she'd been grateful the place didn't possess anything resembling a broom closet.

Ethan sat with his hat on his knees—Georgia courtroom etiquette forbade the wearing of hats in court. The young man next to him must be Sam.

She put them out of her mind. Today was all about making a strong start in her new job. Taking the first step on her road home.

The bailiff called the first case, a rancher representing himself on a DUI rap. The man pleaded not guilty on the grounds he'd driven in an emergency, taking his dog to the vet. Cynthia pointed out that "emergency" was not a legal defense, and found him guilty.

"Next time, pay for a house call or take a cab to the vet," she ordered, before she revoked his license for a year and fined him five hundred dollars.

Her sentence drew a protest from one of the man's friends. "But, Judge, Ernie never drives drunk—in fact, he's always our designated driver. It was a special circumstance."

"He won't take a taxi," Ernie's wife, Cynthia guessed, said loudly. "It'll be me driving him everywhere, you know that, don't you? He's on the planning committee for the county fair—do you realize how many meetings that involves?"

Cynthia tapped the block with her gavel. "Order." In the city, she'd have looked to the attending police officers to quiet the protest. But the sheriff, leaning against the wall between windows, was nodding in apparent sympathy for the dissenters. *Great.* "Twelve months is the minimum disqualification period specified under Georgia State law," she stated. Maybe she should have mentioned that before she sentenced him—she would learn from the mistake. "If you'd hired a lawyer, you would know that and might have found a more effective defense." She could never understand why people chose to represent themselves.

As the muttering subsided, the clerk announced the next case, a civil hearing for the man who was behind on child support. Cynthia's order for the defendant to make back payments infuriated him—he insisted his ex-wife's new boyfriend was getting the benefit of having the kids around and should pay for the privilege. The ex-wife complained the award was insufficient.

"The state has an appeal process if either party feels it necessary," Cynthia informed them. "This court will not tolerate disputes over rulings." Because if they went on like this, they'd be here forever. And as the only judge in town, the hostility felt personal.

She'd talked through the order of cases with the clerk yesterday, and had set Sam Barrett last, wanting to get a few sentences under her belt. She'd also hoped most of the spectators here to check out the *lady judge* would have got bored and left.

But by the time Sam stepped into the dock, the room was packed. Ethan sat in the front row, where he'd been all morning—scrutinizing her performance?—and now people were patting him on the shoulder, shaking his hand, sympathizing.

Cynthia stifled thoughts of her calm, quiet chambers. And the closet.

Sam pleaded guilty to defacing public property. The D.A. read out reports from the sheriff and the librarian about the damage. Sam had acted alone, attacking the library with a spray can around midnight.

"Ethan Granger has a submission on sentencing," the boy's lawyer said. It wasn't the first time she'd heard those words this morning. An hour earlier, Ethan had been called to comment on a repeat offender who'd punched a hole in a window in a fit of rage. Every woman in the courthouse, young or old, had been riveted on him, Cynthia noticed. She'd made notes while he spoke, mainly to give herself a reason not to look at him.

She glanced down at those notes now. Ethan had made the compelling point that the window-punching boy would struggle to control his temper as long as his home environment included his two older brothers, both with a track record of violence. She'd sentenced the youth to Ethan's work program on the recommendation of the parole officer. But she still wanted to know more about the payment Ethan received for the program.

The bailiff invited Ethan to the front of the courtroom. As before, he took the witness stand to make his submission. Cynthia allowed herself a proper look at him. He wore a pale gray shirt with a darker gray tie—entirely suitable for court, but it didn't mask his strong physique.

"Your Honor." He gripped the stand with a tension she hadn't seen earlier. "Sam is an intelligent young man who's had some major upheaval in his life. He needs the support of family around him, and a focus for his considerable energy. Working at the Double T ranch will address those issues."

The mood in the courtroom was unmistakably in his favor. Cynthia started to feel beleaguered. Instead of simply declaring her sentence as she was entitled to, maybe she should take people through her decision process.

She leaned toward her microphone. "Mr. Granger, could you clarify for the court the exact nature of your relationship to Sam Barrett."

He blinked. "He's my son. You know that."

Yes, but it has to be on the record. "So if Sam served his community service on your ranch, he would be working at home. With his father."

In the dock, Sam twitched.

"If this is about the money, Your Honor," Ethan said slowly, "I wouldn't expect to be compensated."

That he even had to say that was an indication of how weird the situation was—she had grounds to refuse his request right there. But the locals were nodding approval; it seemed they couldn't see the problem.

"Mr. Granger, how did you feel when you heard Sam had been arrested for vandalism?"

Ethan flexed his fingers on the witness stand rail. "What do you mean, how did I feel?"

"Were you angry?"

Ethan shot a look at Sam's lawyer.

"Uh, Your Honor..." the lawyer said. Unsure how far he wanted to antagonize the new judge.

She quelled him with her stare. "Mr. Granger?"

"I was disappointed," Ethan said in a low voice.

She waited, but that was all he was offering. "Not angry?"

"No."

"The reason I ask is because it's difficult to be objective about one's own family." She was trying, subtly, to remind him that yesterday he'd said Sam despised him, that he couldn't get through to the kid.

"I don't anticipate any difficulty," he said. "My work program has proven effective for other young people..."

"You betcha," someone called.

"...and it'll do the same for Sam."

"It will also put him in close proximity to other troubled youths, who could be a harmful influence," Cynthia pointed out.

His eyes narrowed at her reference to his own suggestion that Sam had been unduly influenced. "Does Sam get to work at the Double T, or not?" His voice was tight, flinty.

A rumble of chatter, too indistinct for one offender to be singled out, started near the front row, then worked its way back. The sheriff shifted on his feet.

"Thank you for your submission, Mr. Granger, you may leave the stand."

Ethan didn't return to his seat. Instead he sat at the lawyer's table. The bailiff didn't pick up on the breach of protocol, so Cynthia let it go. She scrutinized Sam. A definite resemblance to Ethan—the same dark hair, same stubborn chin. But Sam's eyes weren't as dark. His build was slighter than his dad's, longer in the torso and shorter in the legs. A good-looking young man, who doubtless set hearts aflutter in school.

A young man set for trouble, judging by the three arrests since he arrived in town. His expression had grown increasingly sullen as he listened to his father.

She pinched the bridge of her nose. This shouldn't be so hard. Maybe she wasn't cut out to be a judge after all. *Pull yourself together.* She rested her forearms on the bench, one hand over the other. *I can do this.*

"Sam," she said, "do you think working on your father's ranch is an appropriate sentence?"

A flurry of reactions around the room told her people had expected her to do whatever Ethan recommended.

"No," the teenager said. "He's mad at me, and I don't want to work with him."

"Sam," Ethan began, "I'm not mad."

"Mr. Granger, you will speak when the court addresses you," Cynthia said in her best judge voice. Someone gasped. Too bad. "Sam, it seems to me you need to occupy your time better during the day, so that you're too tired to skulk around at midnight with a spray can."

Relief crossed Ethan's face, in inverse proportion to the consternation on Sam's. *Not so fast.*

"I believe it is in Sam's interest to be separated from other youths who might share the same tendency to damage public property," she said, addressing the court. "I also believe it will be difficult for Mr. Granger to manage his son in the work program."

Ethan looked as if he wanted to raise a strenuous objection. When the lawyer put a hand on his arm, he clenched his jaw.

"My preference is for sentencing that reflects the nature of the crime and if possible makes restitution," she continued, her confidence growing. She might be new to judging, but over the years she'd thought a lot about how to make sentences more meaningful and effective, while preventing offenders from becoming more hardened in their ways. Especially young offenders. "We need to take into account the need for justice, for both victim and offender. We do not need to take into account the needs of the offender's father."

Ethan glowered.

"Samuel Barrett, you have been found guilty of vandalism. I sentence you to one hundred hours of community work, to include the removal of your graffiti from the library building and then working with the librarian on whatever tasks she assigns to you."

The librarian, sitting at the far end of the front row, dropped her knitting. "I don't want that lout near my books." She subsided under Cynthia's stare.

"Your Honor, this is a bad idea." Ethan, who else?

"Mr. Granger, if you can't respect the decision of this court, I will find you in contempt, an offence that carries a short but effective jail sentence."

She hadn't exactly intended to threaten the most respected man in town, but that was the way it came out. A belligerent rumble rolled around the courtroom. The sheriff's hand went to his gun. Just what she needed, insurrection on her first day. Sam's snicker didn't help; she glared at him.

"I know what's best for my son." Ethan's deep voice drew her attention. Hostility emanated from him in waves. Just when she thought he might start yelling, he wheeled around and left the courtroom.

Cynthia realized Jim, the clerk, was talking in a low voice. "That's it for the morning, Your Honor."

"We'll stand in recess until 1 p.m.," she announced, her voice too high. She stood, and the bailiff belatedly caught up with an "All rise."

She forced herself to take measured steps through the judge's exit, to ignore the resentment aimed at her. As soon as the door closed behind her, she practically ran up the back staircase to her chambers. She sank into her chair.

"It's easy for you to wave your sword and hold your scales," Cynthia grumbled to Justice, standing faithfully on the mantelpiece. "That blindfold means you can't see that everyone hates you." Her gaze drifted farther, to the closet. She swiveled her chair to face the window.

She didn't want to think how her father would have rated her performance today. She thought about calling Megan to confide just how difficult it had been. But she wasn't sure she could hold herself together and sound as if she was de-stressing the way she should be.

How long before she could leave Stonewall Hollow and go back home? And what were the odds that she'd be completely crazy by the time she got out of here?

Cynthia's cell phone rang as she unlocked the front door of her cottage the following evening. She pressed to answer. "Hi, Dad."

"Cynthia." Her father always boomed into cell phones; she held the phone a couple of inches from her ear. "I meant to call last night, but it was the golf club banquet. How was your first day in court—your first two days?"

She kicked her shoes off as she closed the door. The house was a few minutes' walk from the court—she'd chosen it from the Realtor's list with a vague vision of her newly relaxed self strolling to work each day in smog-free air—and her feet were sore. The carpet, faded and soft, welcomed her bare toes. "It was okay."

Silence. Her father expected firmer sentiments. How could she have forgotten that just a few days out of Atlanta? "I heard twenty-eight cases yesterday, thirty-four today," she said. Today had gone better—lots of muttering, but the sheriff didn't finger his gun once. "Nothing more complicated than a DUI, I'll speed up with practice."

Sam Barrett's case had been full of complications, none of them legal.

"I struck an unusual interpretation of the law on criminal trespass," she said, looking for something that might interest her dad. "The attorney tried to argue his client was authorized to enter a car lot after hours because the firm's radio advertisement said, 'Come on down today.'"

Her dad laughed. "Sounds like he got his degree out of a cereal packet."

"What's striking is that the D.A. didn't argue unlawful purpose—I had to do it for him." The D.A. hadn't appreciated her prompting, but the law was the law.

With each word, her tension dripped away and the weight in Cynthia's chest lightened. She stopped pacing the small living room—

no open-plan renovation for this cottage—and settled onto the faded gold corduroy couch. Feet curled beneath her, she ran through a few more cases.

"You're doing a great job, as I knew you would," her father said. "What about the... other thing?"

It wasn't like him to be so abstract. Her meltdown had left him nonplussed in a way she'd never seen him.

"I'm fine, Dad." No need to tell him about the closet in her chambers. "I'll be ready to come back to Atlanta in no time."

"Hmm."

Resentment constricted her chest. All those years of being the perfect daughter, then one slip and she was out of town.

Because Dad wants the best for me.

The same thing she wanted for herself.

"What's new with Megan and Sabrina?" she asked.

"Cynthia, you've only been gone three days. What could be new?" Jonah chuckled. "How are you getting along with the locals?"

The question was well out of his usual sphere of interest. She frowned as she traced a knot in the pine coffee table with her finger. "Okay, I guess."

This time, he didn't notice her lackluster response. "I heard some good news today. Gus Fisher is about to announce his retirement."

Cynthia uncurled her legs. Augustus Fisher was a judge in the Atlanta's Fulton County superior court.

"You could replace him," Jonah said.

He wasn't reluctant to have her home, after all. He was just preoccupied. She scrambled to her feet. "I can't imagine I'm a serious prospect." Worry, not modesty, prompted her.

"Thanks to your leaving town, the whispers have already died down."

She tightened her grip on the phone.

"The powers-that-be are keen to appoint a judge who's sensitive to the concerns of smaller communities," her dad continued. "Some lobby groups have been complaining that the judiciary is full of city lawyers who are out of touch with a big chunk of the population."

"The small-town attitude takes some getting used to," she agreed with feeling. "People approach me openly to talk about sentencing."

"Your experience there will look good on your résumé."

"I won't be here long enough for it to make much difference." She hoped.

A gusty sigh escaped him, and she imagined him settling deeper into the chair in his study. "You can talk up the experience when you need to."

"Dad..." Reluctantly, Cynthia prepared to confess. "Things aren't going so well in court. I mean, I know my decisions are legally sound. But I don't think there's one person in town who agrees with me. No one except me has any objectivity."

"It's often that way when everyone knows everyone," Jonah said. "Trust me, Cynthia. If you want to leapfrog the line into the superior court, you need to get in sync with the locals. Demonstrate that you understand their lives and their issues. In fact—" his voice changed and she imagined him hunching forward to make his point "—you should be doing that anyway. It'll help you win cooperation in the courtroom."

She found it hard to converse on any topic other than work, and she had the lack of a social life to prove it. Her recent disgrace just made it harder. How could she hope to get in sync with anyone, let alone find the kind of long-term relationship both her sisters had, when she was wound tight as a spring?

But as always, her father had a point. Maybe she could use her stint in Stonewall Hollow to practice her rusty social skills. If she messed up, no one in Atlanta would know.

"Dad, you're right about getting in with the locals." She glanced at her watch. "I'm going to start right now. There's a potluck supper tonight—I'll go along."

"That's my girl, never lets anything get in the way of her career."

"Wish me luck," she said.

"You don't need luck, you'll do a great job." He paused. "Cynthia, although it's important to integrate with the town, make sure you don't let anyone have undue influence."

For some reason, she pictured Ethan Granger in court yesterday, his eyes hard, his mouth clamped shut as if his silence would stop her noticing his resentment. "Don't worry, Dad. I won't."

Chapter Four

Getting ready for the potluck was much harder than getting ready for a state banquet. Cynthia discarded every single item of the limited casual clothing she'd brought with her before settling on a sundress of Sabrina's. Sabrina had worn it once, back when she was Miss Georgia, to face the media when she was booted out of the Miss U.S.A. pageant. Afterward, she'd told Cynthia she wouldn't be able to wear it again without thinking of one of the worst days of her life.

It fit a little more snugly on Cynthia than it had on Sabrina, but it was fine. She rubbed the filmy yellow fabric between her fingers as she paused outside the museum and community hall complex. This was the perfect dress to say *Cynthia Merritt, girl around town,* rather than *Judge Cynthia Merritt,* but she was overly conscious of her bare shoulders beneath the spaghetti straps. *It's practical,* she told herself. It had to be eighty degrees still, and the humidity made it feel hotter.

She wiped her palms on the floaty skirt and pondered the mystery that she could walk into a high-profile murder trial with absolute confidence, but fret about the possibility of failure at a potluck. Then she pushed the door open.

The pastor was saying grace. When the door banged behind her, at least twenty people looked up. Cynthia closed her eyes for the remainder of the prayer, which was considerably longer than any grace she'd ever heard.

Behind her, someone else slipped in, far more quietly than she had, and waited next to her.

At last the preacher said, "Amen."

Cynthia opened her eyes. And discovered Ethan standing beside her. What were the odds the hundred or so people in the room were frowning at *him?*

"Hey, Ethan." Ernie Rice, the man she'd sentenced on the DUI charge, ignored her.

She resisted the urge to ask him if his wife had driven tonight.

"Good evening, Mr. Granger," she said politely.

Ethan's grunt might have been a hello.

She registered Sam's presence, right behind his father. *Great.* The night was clearly going to be one of courthouse déjà vu, a game she sometimes played with Megan when they attended a swanky function—name which guest has appeared in court and why. "Hello, Sam."

He nodded.

"Speak up," Ethan told him.

This time, she got a mumble. Still, his father hadn't set a great example.

Melanie made her way over. "I'm so glad you made it, Cynthia." She pressed a glass of tea into Cynthia's hand. "There are at least eight different kinds of barbecue, and the desserts…" She circled her finger and thumb and kissed them theatrically. "To die for."

Ethan walked away—he was immediately surrounded by people, almost clamoring to talk to him. No wonder the man had big ideas about how much influence he should wield in the court.

Melanie introduced Cynthia to her sister, Margaret.

"Mellie and I are the spinster sisters of Stonewall Hollow," Margaret announced, double gold hoops bobbing in her earlobes as she pumped Cynthia's free hand. "No man brave enough to take us on. Not for long, anyway. Let me introduce you to some folks, Judge."

Respect for Cynthia's position—or maybe it was just affection for the sisters—scored her a dozen handshakes. Beyond that, stiff words and forced smiles, before people moved swiftly on. Whatever happened to small-town hospitality? "It's so nice to meet you, I'm delighted to be here," she said in a dozen different ways. Didn't matter how she said it—she still got the cold treatment. Half these people hadn't even been in the courtroom, but every one of them had heard how she went against the mighty Ethan Granger.

When she'd exhausted her stock of synonyms for *delighted,* and she no longer had the strength to smile, she joined the line at the buffet.

"This all looks so good," she said to no one in particular. So much for using tonight to brush up her social skills. She piled a spoonful of cheesy grits onto her plate and added some collard greens. Hearty Southern fare. When she'd heaped the plate with more food than she could ever eat, she could no longer procrastinate. She scanned the clusters of plastic seats around the room for someone who wouldn't move away when she sat next to them.

Melanie was engrossed in conversation. She at least had conceded Cynthia's courage in defying Ethan, and Cynthia would be welcome to join her and Margaret, but she could hardly fasten herself to her administrative assistant like a barnacle.

She bit her lip. Good grief, this wasn't elementary school. She was a grown woman who could sit wherever she chose. Including over there, with that group of seniors. Older people were intrinsically polite, weren't they?

"Hi, I'm Cynthia Merritt," she said to a man sporting a prominent hearing aid as she slipped into the seat next to his.

"Hello, Judge," he replied. So there was no need to explain why she was in town. Thankfully, his companions all returned her greeting. She did her best to store their names. Silence settled, as they looked at her expectantly. About now, Sabrina would say something charming and amusing to put everyone at ease.

Cynthia dug a fork into her grits.

Ethan listened with only half an ear to Joe Cates's description of the truck he planned to buy in Albany. Yet again, his gaze was drawn to the new judge. Who would have thought she'd look so young, so girlish, in a sundress? *I would have,* he admitted irritably. Yep, the judge had been on his mind pretty much non-stop the past two days. He alternated between unsought recall of her pretty face and curvy figure, and being hopping mad about the way she'd ignored his advice and sent Sam to work in the damn library.

If she'd bothered to learn the first thing about how folks thought around here...look at her, acting as if chatting to those old people was some Herculean task, her eyes wide and desperate. No doubt she was spouting off about justice, when all they wanted was someone to hear them out on the parlous state of today's youth.

She needed to learn towns like Stonewall Hollow were a lot more personal than the city...though she'd likely figured that out when she was dealt the cold shoulder during Melanie's introductions tonight. Much as he appreciated folks' loyalty, he felt a twinge of sympathy.

Quit thinking about the judge. Ethan turned away, and caught sight of his mom talking to the sheriff. She'd be poking her nose into his and Sam's business—she had no right to play the concerned grandmother after the kind of mother she'd been.

He tipped his head back, blocking his mother out, too, but there was only so long he could stare at the ceiling without Joe breaking off to sympathize about his "problem" son. On balance, he'd rather look at the judge.

Some of the people Cynthia had been talking with had gone for dessert. The last two, Mr. and Mrs. Hobbs, were summoned by a friend as Ethan watched—they got up and left her alone. Head high, a small smile on her lips, she scanned the room. *Not my problem.*

Ethan flexed his fingers, still sore from the blisters he'd earned taking out his frustration on the woodpile around the back of the house after Sam's hearing yesterday. Another black mark against the judge. No one else had come close to provoking his temper. Even with Sam, whose entire purpose in life was to drive Ethan crazy, he managed to hold on to his hard-won calm.

At least Sam's behavior was fueled by some valid resentment. Ethan could understand it. The judge was just plain ornery, and didn't care what her attitude was doing to his family.

Cynthia's smile faltered. Quickly, she pinned

it back in place. Why had she even showed up? He'd been certain she wasn't interested in getting to know them. He'd bet money the judge had never been to a potluck in her life. She had the stamp of Atlanta's privileged classes all over her, from her smooth, glossy blond hair down to the high-heeled sandals on her slim feet.

Out of the corner of his eye, Ethan saw his mom walking purposefully in his and Joe's direction, her hands twisting at her sides in that nervous way they did when she had to deal with something unpleasant.

"Dammit," he muttered. He excused himself as he jammed his sore fingers in his pockets and headed for the judge. It would be a good test of his self-restraint, he told himself. If he could keep his cool with her, he could handle anything Sam threw at him.

"Can I offer you a tour of Stonewall Hollow's famous dessert table, Your Honor?"

She started. "Mr. Granger, uh, hi. Were you talking to me?"

Ethan nodded. "Let me take that plate for you." She hadn't finished her meal. He suspected she'd lost her appetite.

She examined him with those gray eyes, as if she could see right into his head, read his motives.

"Dessert was a one-time offer for a limited period," he warned.

She glanced around the room a last time, accepted her dearth of conversational choices. "Then I accept."

He wasn't used to women accepting him out of desperation. He found himself smiling as he deposited their plates on a trolley. He tugged his mouth back into line; he was still mad at the judge.

An audible buzz of conversation rose when Cynthia walked with him to the dessert table. His mom stopped in her tracks. Mission accomplished.

"I can recommend Melanie's pecan pie," he said. "Louisa Allen's ginger cake is hard to pass up, too. It was runner-up at last year's county fair." He indicated the fragrant cake, plump with pieces of stem ginger.

"Not this particular cake, I hope."

This time, he allowed the smile. "I think she baked a new one."

Cynthia took the bowl he handed her and served herself a piece of both the pie and the cake. She moved farther down the table. Ethan went around the other side on a quest for chocolate brownies. Her eyes, direct and clear, met his over the desserts.

"Are you being nice because you want me to do things your way in court?" she asked.

He paused midway through transferring the brownie to his plate. "You're determined to believe the worst of me." At least she was upfront about it. If he was going to stand accused, let it be open rather than veiled resentment. Which didn't mean he would let her get away with it. "I felt sorry for you," he said.

"Oh." Color stained her cheeks.

Yeah, well, she started it. Ethan winced. Sam probably thought the same way—childishly—except Ethan didn't have the excuse of being eighteen years old.

"I don't need your pity."

He wasn't about to comment on that, when it was obvious she needed all the help she could get. "You have enough there?"

She'd added blueberry pie and peach cobbler to her serving.

"I like dessert." She held the bowl close to her chest, shielding it with one hand.

He found himself assessing her curves. Again. Obviously, he didn't get out enough. He nabbed another brownie, found a couple of spoons, then led her to the seating below the stage.

"How did Sam's day go at the library?" she asked.

She had guts, the judge, she didn't shirk trouble. One-handed, Ethan separated a couple of chairs that had their legs tangled. "It took him most of the day to clean up the graffiti." Sam hadn't told him that, of course. Sheriff Davis had filled him in.

She sat down, accepted a spoon from him. "I hope the librarian—Mrs. Gibson, wasn't it?—was pleased to have her building restored."

The brownie smelled of warm chocolate and nuts. "I guess it's tomorrow she's worried about." He took a bite.

"She must have plenty of work for Sam. Shelving books and the like."

"Fran was mugged a couple of years ago. She's been jittery around teenage boys since," Ethan said. "Sam's hundred hours will punish her as much as him." Since Cynthia was so keen on telling it like it is.

Her plate almost slid off her lap before she caught it. "I didn't—surely, since Sam's your son and everyone likes you so much…"

"Wouldn't matter who he is. Which I'd have told you if you'd discussed sentencing with me."

She swallowed. "I'll have his community service redirected."

"To my place."

She took her time spooning up some blueberry pie. "To somewhere equally fitting his crime, where he's working for someone impartial."

Dammit, three months ago Ethan's life had been exactly how he wanted it. Now, everything had gone haywire and he didn't get a say in fixing it. It was enough to drive a guy to—*Proving my self-restraint.* He shifted in his seat, loosened his grip on the spoon.

"Do you plan to leave me here alone now that you didn't get what you want?" she asked coolly.

He was tempted. But if she held all the power, he had to take every opportunity to persuade her to his point of view about Sam.

He realized he hadn't seen his son in a while. He combed the room, found him with Rob Barnes and another kid. Harmless enough. Sam caught him looking, though, and glared.

"I'm not going anywhere," he said. If he'd blinked, he would have missed the barely perceptible slump of Cynthia's shoulders. *Interesting.* Maybe she didn't have quite *all* the power.

She was seriously bothered that no one wanted to talk to her. How could he turn that to his advantage?

Cynthia turned to observe the crowd, her features relaxed, as if she hadn't just betrayed her apprehension. *Too late, Judge.* "Who's the woman with the camera?" she asked. "I think she took my photo."

It took Ethan a moment to find who she meant. "That's Tania Leach, from the *Stonewall Hollow Gazette.* She'll probably want to interview you at some stage. She's harmless enough, so long as you don't ruffle her feathers." He paused. "Think you can manage that?"

Her head snapped around. "Of course I can."

"I wasn't the only one not happy in court yesterday," he pointed out. "From the reception you got here tonight, I'm guessing today didn't go much better."

With her spoon, she carved out a piece of peach cobbler. "It's hardly surprising your friends should take your side."

"We're loyal to our own," he agreed. "Mind you, I've only been here going on twelve years, which makes me a relative newcomer. But I decided this community was worth being part of, and I worked to make it happen." He watched her put the cobbler in her mouth. A crumb remained on her bottom lip.

"I can't worry about people's sensitivities." Her tongue flicked out to round up that crumb, and it took him a moment to process her comment.

"Maybe if you considered their sensitivities, or at least what makes them tick, you wouldn't have had so much trouble," he suggested.

"This isn't kindergarten," she said. "It's the law, and it'll get worse before it gets better—wait till I start sending people's buddies to jail." She started to let out a sigh, but pressed her lips together. One of the straps of her dress slipped down her shoulder. The creamy skin held his attention until she tugged the strap into place.

"If it's any consolation—" not that she deserved consoling "—the sheriff's been trying to catch Ernie driving under the influence for over a year. He'd have hated for you to let him off."

"He might have been more supportive in court," she said indignantly.

"Lonely at the top, huh?" Ethan worked hard to inject sympathy into the question. She'd accused him of being nice to get his own way—maybe that was exactly what he should be doing. If it came down to the judge against the entire town, she might welcome any ally she could get. Even him.

"Uh-huh." She was so busy giving the sheriff the evil eye, she didn't seem to register his question.

"So, Cynthia…" Her eyebrows shot up at his use of her first name. "I said you could call me Ethan," he reminded her.

She gave him a small nod. "I'll allow it," she said, as if they were in court.

"Anyone call you Cindy?"

"No." Laden with warning.

He smiled. "How old are you?"

"What kind of question is that?" She was practically squinting with suspicion.

"It's just, you seem young to be a judge."

"Age has nothing to do with it," she said haughtily. "Judges are chosen on ability."

Which meant she was worried he would think she was too young. "I'm thirty-six," he offered, in a spirit of openness.

"*I* didn't ask."

He grinned, and it coaxed a return smile out of her. Their eyes met, and there was a moment of fragile connection.

"Thirty-two," she said abruptly.

About what he'd guessed. "How long have you been a judge?" Had to be at least a couple of years, if the certainty she'd displayed in the courtroom and her refusal to debate—

Hold on a moment. The judge had developed a sudden renewed interest in the peach cobbler.

"Is this your first time?" he demanded.

She appeared to be giving her mouthful of cobbler the full thirty-two chews recommended for healthy digestion. At last, she swallowed. "Yes, as a matter of fact, this is my first judicial appointment."

"I don't believe it," he said, outraged. "My son's up in court, and they send a-a *dude* judge." He checked on Sam, found him still with the same kids.

She darted a quick glance around, then leaned into him. "I am a legal professional, fully qualified to be a judge," she muttered.

"Except for your total lack of experience."

"I've had nearly ten years in the courtroom, Mr. Granger. That's ten more than you. You may be a hero in this hick town—" her eyelids flickered as she realized what she'd said "—but don't think for one second you know my job better than I do." She was close, her breath shallow but urgent. Fleetingly, he wondered how she'd taste—he imagined ginger and peach.

Could his libido please stay the hell out of this? "Don't think for one second I'll let you get away with incompetence," he said roughly.

Was it his imagination, or did she pale?

"Coffee, you two?" Melanie chirped. The tray she carried held half a dozen coffees.

Ethan talked his temper down as he took a mug for himself, one for Cynthia. "How do you like yours, Your Honor?" he said evenly.

"Black with one sugar, thank you, Mr. Granger." The color was back in her cheeks.

"Come on, guys," Melanie chided them. "I saw your cozy little tête-à-tête just now. You can't tell me you haven't gotten past the formalities."

"You're right," Ethan said, "*Cynthia* and I were just talking about—"

"Hobbies," Cynthia interjected. She stood very still, as if she was holding her breath.

Ethan left her hanging as he sweetened and stirred both their coffees. He handed Cynthia hers. "Hobbies," he agreed, lengthening his drawl for full effect, since *hick* was the flavor du jour. "Mine are cow-wrangling and poker."

"Amazing," she said briskly, "so are mine."

She came back fighting every time. And, bizarrely, it made him want to laugh. Clearly an overreaction to stress.

"I'm glad you two are getting along." Melanie's complacency said she meant more than a judge getting along with a guy who ran a community service program.

No way. No matter what his hormones thought about her mouth and how she'd taste.

On the other hand, Cynthia looked positively wretched as she sipped her coffee. As if she wanted to set Melanie straight, but didn't want to give Ethan an opening to share his thoughts concerning her professional abilities.

He wasn't about to accuse her of incompetence without thinking it through. He needed to act in Sam's best interests. For now, he would settle for making her as uncomfortable as he could.

"Yeah, Judge Cynthia is pretty cute," he said to Melanie. "Even cuter than the triplet calves my prize cow gave birth to last week."

Cynthia sputtered on her drink.

"Careful." He took the mug from her. "Do you make a habit of spilling coffee?"

Her eyes flared, and color rose in her face. So, she was still embarrassed about being found in the closet. Now that he knew she was a brand-new judge, he wondered if she really had been accidentally shut in there, or…

"Triplet calves are very rare," Melanie reassured Cynthia. "They're quite unique. And as Ethan says, very cute."

Now Cynthia looked flustered, as if she wasn't used to receiving compliments, bovine or otherwise. Which he found hard to believe.

"While it's very kind of you to compare me to your cattle—" she lied barefacedly, he noted with interest "—in view of our professional relationship, perhaps we should avoid such personal remarks."

Melanie looked disappointed.

"Whatever you say, Your Honor."

For now.

Chapter Five

Ethan phoned Cynthia at work several times over the next few days. Each time, she panicked at the sound of his voice.

Not that she couldn't handle a man who pretended to be sympathetic, then pounced at the first sign of weakness. That was standard courtroom practice, a technique she'd used more times than she could count. But she'd never had the added complication of such—such excessive *awareness* of her opponent. Maybe that was why courtrooms had benches and docks and witness boxes—physical barriers between antagonists.

Because when she'd gotten close to Ethan

at the potluck, telling him in no uncertain terms she was more than qualified for this job, she'd had only half her mind on what she was saying. The other half, doubtless the same half responsible for emotional meltdowns and broom closet incidents, had reeled under the masculinity he exuded. Had taken note of such irrelevancies as his hard-planed cheekbones, his strong chin, his— No, she hadn't stared at his mouth. That would've been inappropriate.

His first call, the morning after the potluck, was an unexpectedly friendly invitation to inspect the work program on his ranch; Cynthia declined on the grounds she was snowed under at work. She kept her response calm and measured.

The next day, he phoned with suggestions about a couple of defendants on her docket; she duly noted them and thanked him. He made some self-deprecating remark that piqued her suspicions. His objections to her couldn't have evaporated...but she made her goodbye warmly professional.

Friday afternoon, she received a further request that she transfer Sam's community service to the ranch. Cynthia refused, politely reiterating the reasons she'd given in court, which she was under no obligation to do. Heavy silence followed. She wasn't surprised the faux-friendliness had gone, now they were on Ethan's real agenda. She half expected him to launch into a complaint about her lack of experience, steeled herself to fight back…but he muttered a curt goodbye and hung up.

She didn't hear from him on the weekend, of course. Saturday and Sunday were very quiet, a couple of solitary runs, lots of reading of legal tomes and updates. Let Ethan ask her anything at all about judging—she could give him an answer that would tie him up in knots.

She was almost disappointed he didn't call Monday or Tuesday, prepared as she was. When he phoned Wednesday, it was to invite her, once again, to visit the ranch.

"You need to get out of the courthouse, see some more of the town," he said. "This is an ideal opportunity." It was unsettling the way his voice conjured his image in her mind. Cynthia imagined him on horseback, talking into his cell phone as he squinted into the noon sun, adding to those little lines around his eyes.

"I *need* to get through my caseload," she

replied. It was true—but she was also mindful of her father's warning about letting anyone have undue influence. She didn't think she was so weak as to let Ethan take advantage of her hyperawareness, but after all that had happened recently, she couldn't be sure.

One of those weighty pauses.

"I recommend you accept my invitation," he said.

"Are you threatening me?" Because there was definite menace underlying those innocuous words. She pulled the phone from her ear and glared at it. When she listened in again, she caught the tail end of a sentence: "...good experience for you."

"There's nothing wrong with my experience," she snapped, and ended the call.

She hoped he fell off his damn horse.

Ethan's "threat" niggled at Cynthia the rest of the day, which was probably what he'd intended. Not that she was afraid of him, but she didn't want him bad-mouthing her around town. Though he'd had plenty of opportunity to do that since the potluck, and there was no indication he'd said anything...

"Forget him," she muttered as she pulled a pack of store-bought lasagna from the freezer on Wednesday night. She put the lasagna in the microwave and set the timer. The machine whirred into life.

Her relationship with the town was going to hell in a handbasket without Ethan's "help." Sometimes it felt as if she spoke a different language, and the more she tried to explain her decisions, the less people understood.

But she had a chance to change that. Right after she'd talked to Ethan today, the journalist she'd seen at the potluck, Tania Leach from the weekly *Stonewall Hollow Gazette,* had called to say she was writing a profile of Cynthia and requested they meet.

A fantastic PR opportunity, one she intended to take full advantage of. She hadn't done many media interviews as a lawyer, beyond the traditional posttrial soundbites on the courthouse steps, but Sabrina had the media wrapped around her little finger. Cynthia glanced at the microwave—ten minutes left for her lasagna, just enough time to call her sister.

"A profile, just about you?" Sabrina asked doubtfully, when Cynthia explained.

"Why not? I'm the first *lady judge* around here. The reporter's coming to my chambers Friday lunchtime."

"The longer the article, the more the reporter needs to research you so she can meet her word count," Sabrina warned. "There's a greater chance something you don't like will make it into the paper. When I was Miss Georgia, the short news items were mostly okay. But whenever a magazine profiled me, all that ancient history about my accident and the feud between me and Jake came out."

Cynthia put a plate in the oven to warm, and laid the table. "I wouldn't want *everything* to be in the article," she admitted. She didn't have to specify the broom closet.

"Then pull in some other people," Sabrina advised. "Make it a team profile or an issue profile—these days I only do interviews if they're about education for injured kids." Sabrina was spokesperson for the Injured Kids Education Trust. "Take the heat off yourself."

Galling though it was, her baby sister was right. First thing next morning, Cynthia told Tania, the journalist, she would only participate if the profile focused on the town's crackdown on crime. For that they'd need the mayor and the sheriff, too. The reporter didn't sound happy, but she agreed.

Cynthia hung up the phone satisfied she'd done everything possible to make sure the article came out right.

* * *

"Judge Merritt, if you could stand directly beneath the town crest," Tania Leach suggested. "Then the mayor to your left, sheriff to the right."

"No problem," Mayor Larsen said. He moved into place, beneath the crest that hung in the lobby of city hall.

Sheriff Davis came around the other side of Cynthia. Perfect, she thought. The photo would show better than a thousand words that she and the town's elected leaders were on the same side. Mayor Larsen had been delighted to join in on the article—he'd made no secret of the fact he'd been fielding complaints about her the past week and was keen to "put things in perspective."

Thankfully, though people might complain all they wanted, the mayor had no jurisdiction over Cynthia.

"That's great." Tania snapped a couple of pictures with her digital camera. When Cynthia had been appointed interim attorney general, the *Journal-Constitution*'s political editor had visited her office, and the photo shoot had been a separate event, complete with a change of outfits. She preferred this lower pressure scenario.

When Tania had the shots she needed, they adjourned to the mayor's office for the interview. Richard phoned through to his assistant. "Bring us some tea, could you, Linnet?"

"I'm due back in court at one," Cynthia reminded the reporter.

"This won't take long." Tania set a voice recorder on the mayor's desk. "The feature will appear in the paper the week after next. I've done some background research, but I wanted to talk to you all before I go any further."

"I appreciate the chance to be involved." Cynthia smiled, mindful of Sabrina's advice not to be defensive.

"Judge Merritt, I want to talk about the shake-up you're giving our quiet town," Tania began.

"I'm not sure it's a shake-up," Cynthia said cautiously. But not, she thought, defensively.

Tania flipped the pages in her spiral-bound notebook until she reached a blank one. She picked up her pen. "Your sentencing seems, dare I say it, all over the place. A teenage girl gets a slap on the wrist for shoplifting, while one of our town's prominent businessmen is jailed for a week for contempt of court? People are struggling to make sense of it."

"Ah." Cynthia sat straighter. Jailing Paul

Dayton for contempt wasn't her finest moment, in a judicial career that had so far been light on fine moments. But Dayton was a bully—up on a simple traffic violation, he'd insisted on a jury trial. Then proceeded to intimidate the jury through subtle aggression. Cynthia hadn't been able to think of another solution.

"Courtroom discipline is one of the foundations of an effective legal system," she told the reporter. "Without it, our system doesn't run. Whereas the shoplifter you mention was a first offender, remorseful in the extreme, a model student about to begin her senior year in high school. She didn't need to begin it with a criminal record."

"Judge, you oughta know that Paul is Tania's brother-in-law," Sheriff Davis said.

"Thanks, Sheriff." Cynthia managed not to betray her alarm. She could query the reporter about conflict of interest, but what was the point? As Ethan said, this place thrived on it.

"I stand by my sentence," she told Tania.

"Yet it didn't achieve your goal of discipline in the courtroom," the reporter pointed out. "With Paul yelling, and his family in tears..."

More than tears, they'd been wailing. Although a deputy had intervened, it had been chaos. Cynthia pressed her fingers to her eyes, blotting out the image. Then she dropped her hands and said, "Discipline is an ongoing process, one that ultimately makes the system more effective. Mayor Larsen has some interesting views about how the court serves the needs of the town."

Tania sneered at the attempted distraction. Thankfully, the mayor's assistant arrived bearing a tray with a jug of tea and four glasses. She set it down on the desk. "Shall I pour, Richie?" she asked.

Cynthia didn't want tea, but neither did she want to draw attention to herself by refusing. She accepted a glass with a smile. "Thank you."

And met cold dislike in the assistant's eyes.

Great, another enemy. She didn't know the woman, but doubtless her husband or nephew or cousin had complained about his court hearing. That made it four against one in here. Cynthia considered spilling her tea down her white linen dress and escaping.

But she'd started this, she would see it through.

When everyone had their tea, the assistant sat down with a pen and notepad. The mayor launched into a spiel about business owners' morale and his commitment to ensuring Stonewall Hollow was a safe place to live and work. Cynthia gathered the last election had been close-run; he left no stone unturned in claiming a stake in every successful venture, including some that hadn't happened yet.

"Next week's county fair will be the best ever," he promised.

"I'm sure," Tania said, "but we're here to talk about the town's approach to crime and justice." Just when Cynthia thought she was going to get another grilling about Paul Dayton, the reporter asked Sheriff Davis about the rehabilitation of young offenders. He mentioned Ethan's work program in glowing terms. He didn't seem to have any doubts about it.

"Judge Merritt—" Tania switched back to Cynthia "—you commented in one of your summings-up this week that Stonewall Hollow has a pick-and-choose approach to traffic laws. Which cases were you referring to?"

"That wasn't intended to single anyone out." Cynthia was learning fast that everything was personal around here. "I was describing the prevailing attitude to stop or yield signs. People obey them in the center of town, but as soon as they're away from the main drag, they seem blind to the signs." The journalist frowned. "Folk have wonderful respect for speed limits," Cynthia added positively.

"Mayor Larsen, you were elected on a platform of supporting families." Tania changed tack. "How does jailing Paul Dayton, the upstanding father of five kids, square with that?"

The mayor ran a finger around his collar. "You know I'm not going to comment, Tania." The edge to his voice was directed at Cynthia. He'd visited her chambers after she'd sentenced Dayton, asking her to let the guy out early.

Tania smiled. "If the officials won't comment, I'll have to ask the people. How about you, Linnet, what do you think?"

The assistant didn't look up from her notepad. "I'm sure Judge Merritt knows her job. I wouldn't like to tell her how to do it."

Passive-aggressive, the hardest of all behaviors to counter. It was easy to come down against someone who was negative or just plain wrong. But what could Cynthia say to someone who was "sure" the judge knew her job?

After another half hour of questions, she felt as if she'd spent her lunch hour being pummeled by rocks.

At last Tania capped her pen. "Okay, we're done. My next step will be some man-in-the-street interviews, seeking candid opinions about the direction the town is taking on crime."

Cynthia's stomach flipped. Tania planned to ask people what they thought of her? Then report it in the paper?

She envisaged a headline screaming Judge Merritt Go Home.

If only home wanted her.

She pressed a hand to her middle, suddenly queasy.

As she hurried back to the courthouse, she tried to predict the likelihood of her father, or someone involved in the selection of the new superior court judge, seeing the article, in either printed or electronic form. Maybe they wouldn't think to look… Of course they would. Her dad would hear about the interview from Sabrina; he'd order a copy of the newspaper. And these days, everyone ran an Internet search on prospective employees, and most newspapers seemed to post their content online….

She rubbed her throat as the humid air from outside clashed with the cool of the marble entrance hall. Was there some way she could influence the article? If she could think of someone who might say something nice, and suggest they phone the *Gazette*...

She couldn't think of anyone. Except Ethan saying she was as cute as triplet calves, and that was no help at all.

Her heels clattered on the marble staircase as she stumbled on the top step.

"Cutting it fine," Melanie observed. She held Cynthia's robes out to her.

"Thanks." Cynthia slipped her arms through the holes, adjusted the robes so they sat neatly.

"Take a deep breath," Melanie advised. "You still have two minutes. And they can't start without you."

"That's true," Cynthia said, surprised to find the thought did relax her. Then she remembered the reporter and closed her eyes.

"Drink this." Melanie thrust something cold into her hand.

Iced water. Cynthia sipped. "I don't know where I'd be without you, Melanie. There's not one other person around here who supports me." Too bad her assistant couldn't talk to the reporter, but she'd hardly qualify as an objective observer.

"You don't want to get upset about every little thing people say," her secretary demurred.

She realized Melanie's gaze was fixed

somewhere over her left shoulder, and her color was high. Uh-oh.

"Something's happened," Cynthia guessed. "And I'm not going to like it."

"Uh…it's not really a problem," Melanie said. Her tone said *Yet.*

"Tell me." It couldn't be any worse than a reporter trashing her in the newspaper.

"The clerk at Gonville called to see if we can take a half-dozen jury cases off them next week?" Melanie's voice went up in a question. "Probably just a day's work," she hurried on. "You're getting a reputation as a fast worker." Said encouragingly, in willful ignorance of the fact Cynthia was also getting a reputation as a power-crazed tyrant.

Cynthia gulped more water. "Sure, send them over." At least with the out-of-towners, her every decision didn't get picked over like a chicken carcass. "But that's not the real problem, is it?"

Melanie grimaced. "One other thing… Ethan came by."

Cynthia swallowed her water slowly. "Is this about me visiting his ranch?"

"Maybe we should discuss it later."

Cynthia eyeballed her.

"He, uh, asked me how a citizen goes about filing a complaint."

"A complaint?" Her voice had gone high. "About me? You mean, like those people who complained to the mayor."

"A real complaint," Melanie said reluctantly. "A formal one. To Atlanta."

Chapter Six

Somehow, though her insides crumbled, Cynthia held on to her composure.

"I told him I don't know anything about complaints procedures," Melanie assured her. "Well, I don't...but I wouldn't have told him if I did." She patted her hips nervously. "I know Ethan's not happy with you, but he's usually reasonable. If he knew how hard you work, how important it is to you to do things right..."

"Any citizen has a right to file a complaint," Cynthia said mechanically. "It's a fundamental of our legal system."

Her assistant's soft snort did her heart good.

"He's probably just having a bad day with

Sam," Melanie suggested. "He'll get over it by Monday."

Cynthia nodded even though she didn't believe it.

"You look tired," Melanie said. "You're pushing yourself too hard."

Last time Cynthia did that, she ended up in a broom closet.

"What do you have planned for the weekend?" the older woman continued.

"Catching up on some work," Cynthia said ruefully, as if she'd turned down a dozen invitations for the sake of truth, justice and the Stonewall Hollow way. As if Ethan's *complaint* didn't even feature on her mental landscape.

"Margaret and I plan to hit the town tomorrow night if you'd like to join us. Of course, around here, hitting the town means a few drinks at Joe's Bar, followed by the ten-dollar buffet at the Emerald Dragon. You'll still have your virtue by morning." Melanie sounded disappointed.

The offer tempted Cynthia way more than it should. But she'd already resolved not to cling to her assistant. Even if she had no social life and a career in tatters.

Dammit, she was doing her best, and her best wasn't good enough.

Which meant it was time to try something else.

She used the time it took to drain her water glass to run through her choices.

She could do nothing and hope for the best. She'd never done that in her life.

She could bribe someone to say nice things to the reporter, to counter both that appalling interview and whatever Ethan might say in his complaint. Not illegal in this instance, but immoral. Or, she could let Paul Dayton out of jail early and hope that made up for everything else.

Over her dead body.

Or…

"You probably should go downstairs now, honey. I mean, Judge." Melanie smiled apologetically.

See, she wasn't unlikable, her assistant called her honey. She just hadn't quite connected with the rest of the town. These things took time.

Time she didn't have.

Or, I could deal with Ethan.

"Is Ethan's place nearby?" Cynthia asked.

"The Double T is maybe forty minutes

out. Ethan probably does it in thirty-five. Of course, he'll be in town tonight," Melanie continued. "He and some of the guys play poker at the Stonehouse Friday nights."

Cynthia had figured he was joking when he'd named poker and cow-wrangling as his hobbies. If the poker was true, then so, presumably, was the cow-wrangling. *My future depends on a cow-wrangler's goodwill.*

"But the guys are a little precious about their game," Melanie said. "It's like a religious experience. You're better to wait until Monday."

Monday! Ethan could figure out how to complain about her over the weekend, with a simple search of the Internet. From there, all it would take was one e-mail. One phone call first thing Monday.

"You're right," Cynthia lied, "it can wait." How precious could a poker game be?

Cynthia's interrupting-a-poker-game outfit comprised jeans, a white sleeveless georgette blouse that she knew was too dressy, and an orange bandanna knotted at her throat, to counteract the ruffle down the front of the blouse. She'd bought the bandanna for four dollars at Walgreens on her way home from court. The label promised one-hundred-percent cotton, but the fabric's suspicious sheen hinted at polyester.

Cynthia adjusted the knot in the mirror on her visor one last time. She turned her head to check that the black velvet ribbon still held most of her hair in place. She looked casual-ish, not desperate. About the best she could hope for.

She got out of the car and walked into the Stonehouse. The edge-of-town tavern wasn't a house and wasn't made of stone. Presumably it got its name from the two enormous Stonehenge-style rocks that stood on either side of the narrow parking lot entry. She'd bet a few customers had suffered bumper damage trying to maneuver around them after a few drinks. The building itself was stucco, painted an unfortunate shade of lilac that didn't seem to deter the clientele. The parking lot was full and when Cynthia made it inside, so was the tavern.

Though Stonewall Hollow was a small town, most faces here were unfamiliar. Thank goodness. Women in pairs, clusters of men eyeing them, a few couples, and in the corner behind the door, a bunch of young people who may or may not be legally entitled to drink the beers stacked three deep on the table in front of them. Cynthia glanced away. Her job was to judge, not to make arrests, and she was having enough trouble with that.

It took her a good five minutes to reach the bar through the throng.

"I'm looking for the poker game," she shouted over the jukebox playing "Crazy Little Thing Called Love."

The barkeep slid a coaster across the varnished wood surface. "Drink?"

"No, the poker—okay, a white wine spritzer." It wouldn't hurt to relax a little more before she humiliated herself in front of Ethan. "No ice."

The server looked vaguely disgusted, but he poured fifty-fifty white wine and club soda into a tall glass.

Cynthia handed over a ten. "The poker game?" she asked again, as he counted out her change.

He paused, a five dollar bill suspended above her palm. "Nuh-uh, no girls allowed."

"What about grown women?" she asked sweetly, snatching her five bucks.

"Nope, not them, either." He grinned. "Not with clothes on, leastways."

He was kidding. He had to be. She pulled

a straw from the dispenser and stuck it in her drink, then took a long sip.

She considered pulling rank to get the information she needed—*do you know who I am?*—but then this guy would be mad at her like the rest of the town, and being the butt of everyone's dislike was getting old.

Drink in hand, she moved away from the bar. The canned music switched to a country-and-western song, something about a man whose girl had left so he was falling in love with...*his dog?* Ugh, she must have misheard.

The barkeep might not have told her where the game was, but she'd registered the quick, ceilingward flick of his eyes. Poker was upstairs. She wandered through the room, looking for an exit to a stairwell. She found the bathrooms, the restaurant, the haze-filled poolroom, but no stairs. She had to get behind the bar, to that door beyond the cash register.

Which meant ignoring the Staff Only, No Patrons Allowed sign. As a law-abiding citizen, that went against her instincts, so Cynthia ditched her straw and took a fortifying slug of spritzer before setting her glass back on the bar. Feigning deafness to the bartender's protest, she pushed through the swing gate and headed for the forbidden door.

She wrinkled her nose as she climbed the stairs. Unlike the well-ventilated bar, the hallway smelled of cigarette smoke and beer. On the upper landing, she paused. In the long hallway punctuated by doors, only one stood ajar, a thread of light falling onto the worn red carpet.

With a nod to local custom, Cynthia walked in without knocking.

Half a dozen men—no women, naked or otherwise—sat around a square table, cards in hand. A light hung low over the table and a green baize mat took up much of the surface. At Cynthia's entrance, a couple of the players looked up. Not Ethan, sitting at the far end, intent on his five cards, a sizable stack of chips in front of him. Smoke curled from the ashtray at his left hand—all of them had cigars, she observed. Including Sheriff Davis, trying hard not to notice her.

"Good evening, gentlemen," she said.

"Aw, man." The guy nearest her tossed his cards onto the table facedown. "Who let her in?" He turned around, recognized her and said, "Sorry, Judge."

"Evening, Judge," the man next to him said.

The sheriff gave a casual salute. "There a

problem, Judge Merritt? 'Cause if there's not, the boys don't welcome interference in their game." As if he wasn't one of the six men wishing she was somewhere else.

At least, she assumed Ethan shared the sentiment. He still hadn't looked up. His fingers wrapped around a tumbler of amber liquid. Whiskey? Was he drunk? Too drunk to see reason?

"Mr. Granger," she said.

He picked up his cigar, took a drag, then eyed her through the smoke he blew out. His scrutiny started with the black velvet ribbon in her hair, then moved down.

"Howdy, cowgirl." His reaction to the bandanna. His eyes moved lower.

"Sorry to interrupt." Cynthia managed a tight smile. "But I'd like a word."

"Can it wait until tomorrow?" The sheriff sounded exasperated, as if she'd tried his patience good and proper at today's newspaper interview. He chugged his Bud.

"Now," she said to Ethan.

"This game is the highlight of my week." He held up his glass so the glow from the low-hanging light caught it. "I can forget about the garbage that fills the day and do one simple thing that brings me a great deal of pleasure."

"How touching." She squeezed past a guy with an impressive beer gut and advanced on Ethan.

His eyes narrowed, but that might have been the smoke. "So I'm not inclined to quit the game to talk to you," he explained.

He hadn't actually said no.

"Five minutes," she promised. Behind her, someone sighed.

"A man could miss a lot of poker in five minutes." Ethan took a drink. "How about, whatever it is, Your Honor, you tell me here."

Had she been that difficult to deal with on the phone this past week? Maybe.

"It's confidential." She wondered if he'd told these guys he planned to complain about her. If they'd laughed about her. She pushed her hands into the pockets of her jeans and held his gaze.

He gave one last, longing look at his cards, then put them down. "Talk quietly among yourselves, fellas."

"Sorry to drag you out of your game," Cynthia said when they reached the dimly lit hallway.

"How sorry?" He wore a blue-and-brown plaid shirt with jeans and boots. Nothing special, so it had to be long legal practice that had her gauging the breadth of his shoulders, the muscle of his forearm where his sleeves were rolled up.

"Not that sorry," she admitted.

A smile ghosted across his lips. "Okay, Judge, let's cut to the chase. Melanie told you about my visit to the courthouse."

Cynthia wiped her palms on her jeans. "While you're entitled to complain, I think we should talk about whatever's bothering you first."

"As I recall, I've spoken to you on the phone five times in the past week. Each time, you've brushed me off like a burr off a blanket."

"I—" she pushed out the words stuck in her throat "—I apologize."

He stared hard at her. Then he rubbed his chin. "You do that often?"

"Whenever it's justified." Her dad had taught her to make certain she was right before she spoke. She rarely needed to say sorry.

"In that case, apology accepted." Definite mockery in his tone.

Cynthia ploughed on. "While your irritation with me is perhaps justified—definitely justified," she amended when his chin jutted, "lodging a complaint is an overreaction."

He leaned against the wall, arms folded across his chest. "Uh-huh." Was that amusement?

"It can't be easy having your son in trouble with the law," she sympathized.

Subtly, his stance hardened. "You think?"

"Especially when you run a respected rehabilitation program yourself."

"Respected by everyone except you," he pointed out.

She'd never expected this to be easy. She locked her jaw and said, "But it's important not to let your personal stake cloud your judgment."

His eyes glittered. "So if I'm unhappy with the way you handled my son's case, it's my own fault?"

There was no answer that wouldn't put Cynthia in the wrong. In the silence, music filtered up from the jukebox downstairs: Bruce Springsteen, "Dancing in the Dark." The walls closed in on her; she should have turned a light on before she barged into the card game.

"Seems you've annoyed a lot of people since you arrived in town," Ethan observed. "Sending Paul Dayton to jail was a brave move. I wouldn't be surprised if he lodges a complaint—" a pause "—too."

"I did the right thing," she said stiffly.

"I hear Tania Leach isn't your number one fan, either."

He knew about the newspaper profile. Of course he did, he probably had platoons of loyal fans calling to report her every failure. Cynthia hooked her thumbs through the loops of her jeans. "I admit I had a difficult interview with the *Gazette*."

"Difficult?" He straightened, reached for her bandanna, and tugged one end out from her collar. "I heard it was a disaster."

She flinched, but didn't step back. Using both hands, he spread the orange fabric she'd carefully tucked away, revealing the words printed in the corner: *Welcome to Stonewall Hollow.*

"Cute," he said. "A nice souvenir to take back to Atlanta."

Her hand went to her throat, but when her fingers brushed his, she whisked it away. "I'm not leaving anytime soon." Not until she had enough small community experience to satisfy the superior court selection committee, and not until she could convince her dad her head was in the right place.

"Maybe you won't have a choice." He tucked the bandanna back in.

Cynthia bit down on her cheeks and submitted, while she shuffled through the available strategies. The convince-Ethan-he's-unreasonable option went on the discard pile. "I didn't set out to offend anyone in court. It's important to me to do a good job."

"Two things are important to me," he returned. "My son and my work program. You've implied more than once that my work program is crooked, but you've refused to come see for yourself. You won't give an inch on Sam's community service."

She discarded the idea of explaining herself, too. That would only work with a reasonable person.

"I'm sorry." Apologizing could at least do no harm. "If your work program means as much to you as my job does to me, I understand how angry you must feel."

"I'm not angry," he snapped.

Okay, she was wrong. Apologizing *could* make things worse. She held one last card. Cynthia breathed a prayer and played her ace.

"I'd like to take up your invitation to visit the ranch," she said.

Ethan stilled. *At last.*

"You're right, I should check out your program," she continued. "I'd like to take an objective look, and give you a chance to answer my questions."

He shook his head. "Why are you so panicked about me placing a complaint? I'll bet judges get complaints all the time, and ninety-nine percent of them are ignored. Hell, if I'd thought you'd take it so seriously, I'd have complained a week ago."

"I'm not panicked," she said frostily.

"Panicked enough to grovel to me."

"I'm not—"

"Even if a couple of people complain," he interrupted, "surely you can find a few others to say nice things about you."

"The evidence suggests otherwise," she admitted, glad of the darkness now. Her cheeks felt as if they were on fire. This was humiliating. "Even the mayor's assistant made it plain she doesn't like me today, and I'd never met the woman."

"*Linnet* did?" he said sharply.

"Um...yes." If he said that wasn't possible, because Linnet liked absolutely everyone, Cynthia's mortification would be complete.

But he seemed lost in thought.

"Have you ever needed a second chance, Mr. Granger?"

His head jerked up. "It's Ethan."

"Ethan," she said, "I messed up, I've apologized, I want to start over. I'll visit the ranch, if you'll drop your complaint." Yep, she was groveling.

"What do I get in return?"

"Excuse me?"

"It can't have been easy for you to climb down off your high horse and come here. Which means this complaint is a big deal. If I'm going to drop it, I need more of an…incentive." His eyes settled on her lips.

She fought the temptation to cover her mouth with her fingers. "What kind of incentive?" It came out breathless.

"I want you to seriously reconsider transferring Sam's community service to the ranch."

Cynthia lurched backward as if a bucket of cold water had hit her. "That's blackmail."

"It would be blackmail if I *insisted* you shift Sam to the ranch," he said. "I'm asking you to weigh the options once you've seen my program in action, and make the best decision for Sam."

Every instinct told her she'd made the right call in keeping Sam away from the ranch. Still, she examined the suggestion from all sides. What harm would it do to take a look?

Someone called from the poker room. "Ethan, you done out there?"

Without taking his eyes off her, he raised his voice to reply. "Give me one minute." To Cynthia he said, "Sunday afternoon, three o'clock. Take the Old West Road ten miles, then right onto Picards Line. Look out for the Double T sign."

Sunday? So soon?

She nodded.

"Then we have a deal." He stuck out his hand.

She stared at his strong, blunt fingers. Had she done everything she could to fix the mess she was in?

"I want your support," she blurted.

Ethan's hand closed. "What?"

"This town sees you as some kind of hero. If you act as if you—you like me, your attitude will rub off on other people."

"*Like* you?" He couldn't have sounded more horrified if she'd asked him to marry her. Sabrina had done exactly that: forced a fake engagement on Jake, now her husband, to save her career. Back then, Cynthia had been smugly sure she'd never need to resort to such desperate measures.

This was completely different.

"I mean like me in a collegial sense," she explained. "I want to get to know this town, I want people to give me a chance. They're more likely to do that if you're…warm toward me."

Her face felt like a furnace. Maybe he wouldn't notice.

"Warm," he said slowly, eyes on her cheeks. She should have had ice in that spritzer.

"Nothing drastic," she said with a nonchalance she didn't feel. "Just a friendly attitude, a few smiles, maybe the occasional coffee together in public."

"You're unbelievable," he said. "You come here to beg me not to complain about you, and now you expect me to act as if we're best pals."

"What I've proposed works for both of us. If you want me to reconsider Sam's position…" Adrenaline zipped through her veins. Ethan had accused her of never having done anything wild, but this bizarre negotiation was… *Creative and pragmatic,* she told herself. Excellent qualities in a judge.

Ethan hadn't answered.

"Well?" she said, not as firmly as she'd have liked.

They both shifted, and it put them closer

together. Cynthia didn't want to be the first to back away.

"I don't appreciate being manipulated," he said.

She sensed the prize within reach. Now wasn't the time to feel guilty. "You started it."

He raked a hand through his hair. "If I agree to act...warm...you'll come out to the ranch and consider reassigning Sam."

"Definitely," she agreed, generous in victory.

Did he just inch closer? She could see the weave of his plaid shirt. Or maybe she was just staring. So near, his masculine appeal was overpowering.

A tiny step backward brought her up against the wall. Refusing to show her discomfort, she extended a hand. *Now* they could seal the deal, one that was much more to her satisfaction.

He didn't move. Surely he wouldn't pull out now! She tipped her head back to meet his intense gaze.

"I thought you wanted warm," he said.

"I—yes, in a collegial—"

His lips brushed hers, silencing her. Then before she could react, he came back, kissed her again. For less than a second, but enough for Cynthia to catch the smoky taste of whiskey. Her mouth burned as if lightning had struck.

When the kiss ended, he was so close, she could see shadow where he would shave tomorrow morning.

"That was warm," he said.

She tugged her bandanna away from her throat, sucked in a breath. "You must be drunk."

"You think?" He was looking at her lips.

"Of course." She wiped her fingers across her mouth, but she could still feel the kiss. "How drunk are you?"

He put one hand against the wall, as if he wasn't quite steady. "How drunk do you want me to be?"

Blotto. Pie-eyed. Unable to remember this in the morning. "I don't care how much you drink," she said. "Why don't you get back to your card game? With luck, someone will fleece you."

"There are some things I do as well drunk as sober, *Cindy*." His eyes hadn't budged from her lips.

"Just sober up by Sunday," she said. "And my name's Cynthia. Judge Merritt to you."

She marched down the hallway, and hoped

he wouldn't see her clutch at the newel post as she started down the stairs. It didn't matter that he'd mocked her with that kiss. They'd made a deal, and she would make sure he stuck to it.

The sensation of Ethan's mouth on hers still lingered the next morning as Cynthia drank her coffee. When she caught herself tracing her bottom lip with her tongue, she groaned.

"It was a *tiny* kiss," she muttered into her cup. What was the bet Ethan hadn't even remembered it when he woke up this morning? Hopefully with a filthy hangover. Not that he'd actually seemed that drunk. He'd been steady on his feet, articulate, quick-thinking enough to insist she reconsider Sam's community service.

Maybe he hadn't been drunk at all. She turned the thought over.

In which case, why had he kissed her?

Cynthia analyzed the kiss from every angle, so hard that her head hurt as if she was the one who'd been drinking.

Was it a power play? He'd wanted to show her she didn't get to call all the shots? *Message received,* though she was damned if she'd let him see that.

Maybe he'd kissed her because, like her, he'd felt that inescapable sensual tension in the air. But although Ethan was a man of the land, she doubted he gave in to his elemental instincts on a whim. Besides, he probably had every woman in town after him. She was the one with the sad-sack social life. Which was the only reason she was still thinking about that brief but highly inappropriate kiss.

Impatient with her circling thoughts, she pulled on shorts and a T-shirt to go for a run.

Stonewall Hollow sat on the edge of a plain, the west side of town butting up against wooded hills. In any other direction you saw nothing but sky. Cynthia took a trail she'd tried before through the tree-filled lower slopes. Though she liked running, she did it infrequently enough that it was as much punishment as relaxation. By the time she emerged at the other end of the trail, she was puffing like a chain-smoker. But at least she wasn't thinking about Ethan.

At least, not until she ran past Al's Gas and Food Mart, and saw Sam sweeping the forecourt with a wire broom. His lawyer had mentioned Sam had a vacation job here—he juggled his community service hours around his commitments to Al. The lawyer had tabled a positive character reference from Al in court.

She stopped for a breather. "Hi, Sam." She massaged a stitch in her right side.

He grunted.

"You working today?"

He gave her a pitying look. "I don't sweep this dump for free."

No, she guessed he didn't. "How's your service going over at the park?" He'd been reassigned to work with the town's parks department.

"'Kay."

What would it take to get a decent answer out of him? "I could have you transferred to your dad's place if you'd prefer," she said, in a burst of unjudgeworthy malice.

He blanched. "No way. The park's good."

Cynthia raised her right arm over her head and stretched to her left, in an attempt to get rid of that stitch. "Your dad's trying hard to convince me you should work on the ranch with him. He really wants you around." She realized she sounded wistful, and straightened up. Her situation with her father was nothing like Sam's with Ethan.

Sam eyed her suspiciously. Had he heard that wistfulness?

"I'd better keep moving," she said briskly. "I'll see you tomorrow."

"Uh," he grunted. Then, blurted in alarm, "Why?"

"I'm visiting the ranch, to learn how your dad's program works."

"Is that all?"

Could he somehow know his dad had kissed her? "What other reason could there be?"

"You wouldn't make me work with him, would you?" Sam's hostility toward Ethan seemed extreme.

"Your father seems to care a lot about you."

"You're just like everyone else," the boy said. "He's got you thinking he's wonderful, too."

"I do not." This was a bad idea, arguing with Sam about his dad. Cynthia jogged on the spot. "Gotta go, see you later."

She ran on, her breathing strained, from exertion and from an unpalatable realization. That kiss...had it been a ploy by Ethan to get her on his side, make her think he was "wonderful"? To, as her dad would say, exert undue influence?

She picked up her pace. If Ethan thought she'd be a pushover when she got to the Double T, he'd soon learn he was wrong.

Chapter Seven

Ethan flipped the hash browns in the frying pan. "Make sure your room's tidy, too. She'll be here at three."

"No way, the judge is *not* going into my room." Sam banged the carton he was holding on the counter. Orange juice slopped out the spout. He reached for the washcloth to wipe it up…then Ethan saw the moment he deliberately pulled his hand back, ignoring the mess.

Ethan counted to ten. He picked up the cloth, tossed it so it landed on the spilled juice. "There you go."

After a silent, furious moment, Sam made

a halfhearted effort to clean up. Did every damn thing have to be a battle?

"I don't think Cyn—the judge will go into your room," he said. "But it's been a pigsty all week and it wouldn't hurt to at least clear a path to the bed." He had a feeling Cynthia would look closely at how he and Sam lived, even if she didn't actually do a room inspection.

"Mainly I'll show her what the guys are doing outside," he said, only half to Sam.

Sam made a gagging sound. He poured Crispy Flakes—how could an eighteen-year-old do a day's work on that sugar-laden stuff?—into a bowl, and added a generous splash of orange juice.

"You want some milk with that?" Ethan asked.

"Nope." Sam rattled the cutlery in the drawer more than he needed to find a spoon. He sat at the counter and began to eat. Noisily.

"Did your mom forget to teach you manners?"

"She taught me. I just decided not to use them."

Briefly, Ethan fantasized about dunking Sam's face into his cereal. "You'd better remember those manners for Judge Merritt."

"I'm not here to impress her."

"No need to antagonize her, either."

"You better not be going to ask her to make me work here."

"I'm aware of your views on the subject." *Too bad.*

Sam shoved his bowl across the counter. "Are you going to take an interest in what *I* have planned for the day?"

"You need to be here," Ethan said. "We have company."

"*You* have company." Sam slid off his stool. "All you can talk about is the friggin' judge. Like you think she's hot, or something."

Ethan flipped a couple of hash browns that didn't need flipping. "She's here on business, that's all."

"Then I don't need to play the dutiful son."

"I didn't think you know that game." Ethan meant it as a joke, but it didn't come out that way.

Sam's face darkened. "I'm out of here." He grabbed his keys from the hook by the door.

Ethan wanted to yell. He forced reasonableness into his voice. "Where are you going?"

"To see Gram."

He might have known. Sam was going somewhere no one would argue with him. Ethan's mother wouldn't dream of telling him his behavior was unacceptable. It would be nice to have someone other than the sheriff backing Ethan up, but his mom had always been the last person he could count on.

He broke two eggs into the pan. "You want some of this?"

Sometimes food worked when nothing else did. Sam looked momentarily torn. "Nah, I'll get something at Gram's."

"Be back in time to see Judge Merritt," Ethan ordered.

"Whatever." Sam let the door slam behind him.

Ethan gripped the edge of the stove, his head bowed. He'd started the day with such optimism, having convinced Cynthia to review Sam's sentence and knowing just how to swing that review in his favor. The way he'd envisaged it, Cynthia would be dazzled by his program, impressed by his calm handling of Sam. And she'd send more kids out to the ranch and transfer Sam home for the rest of his current sentence.

Simple.

If Sam cooperated.

If Ethan hadn't blown it by kissing Cynthia.

Dammit, what had possessed him? One minute he'd been astounded at her brazenness, insisting he act warmly toward her after the hostility between them. Next minute, his mind had sprinted miles ahead to what *warm* might conceivably mean…and her mouth had been right there in front of him, and it had been the most logical thing in the world to—

Logic had nothing to do with it. The judge might be sexy and smart, not to mention strong-willed, but she was off-limits. He'd told her conflict of interest was inevitable in a small town, but Ethan didn't need to complicate his situation with Sam any further.

And even without the Sam factor…while Ethan was an upright citizen these days, a stickler for the law like Cynthia wouldn't give him the time of day if she knew the truth about his past.

Keep it simple. No more kissing the judge.

Ethan sighed. With the judge off-limits and his son being difficult, the day stretched before him, flat and unappetizing as—

"Dammit." He pulled the pan off the stove, the eggs a blackened mess. He tipped them onto a plate anyway and sat down to eat. At least the silence didn't throb with antagonism. Halfway through, he shoved the plate away. The charred food wasn't the problem. He'd just realized how he felt about his son not being here.

Relieved.

Cynthia arrived at the Double T fifteen minutes early, not really expecting to find Ethan burying the bodies of exploited workers...but if he was, she might as well turn up in time to catch him red-handed.

She pulled up outside the two-story white clapboard ranch house and switched off the engine. To her right was a dark-stained board and batten barn; Ethan came around the side, a hand raised in greeting.

Wearing jeans with holes in the knees and a T-shirt that molded to his shoulders and chest, a battered straw cowboy hat wedged on his head against the glaring sun, he looked half rancher, half outlaw. She'd convinced herself she'd neutralized the threat he represented. But today he seemed doubly dangerous.

I am a judge. I am not swayed by too-sexy men who steal drunken kisses during poker games. She climbed out of the Volvo and tugged her mint-green tank top down to meet her sky-blue capris.

"Welcome to the Double T, Judge Merritt," he said formally. No reason for her to think of his lips on hers, of that fleeting firmness, overlaid with sensual softness....

Cynthia fanned her face. "It's a scorcher this afternoon."

"You need any sunscreen for those shoulders?"

"I already put some on." She dived back into the car, busied herself spreading the folding shade across her windscreen. Keep it simple. She was here to fulfill her part of the odd bargain they'd struck on Friday night. And sealed with a kiss.

"Let's go." Ethan strode toward the barn. "Sooner we get started, the sooner I get my son back where he belongs."

She ignored the dig. "Is Sam here?" she asked as she caught up with him.

"He had an errand in town. Should be back any minute." Barely breaking his stride, he bent down to pull a weed from between two of the half logs that edged the driveway.

"So, you mostly run cattle here?" Cynthia said, remembering the triplet calves.

"Angus beef," he confirmed, "the best beef you'll find. We grow a few onions, too."

"Onions?" She laughed at the incongruity, and some of her tension eased.

"Award-winning onions," he elaborated.

"You're in Vidalia country here, and ours are some of the best."

They rounded the barn. On this side, double doors stood open. Inside, two young men, one of whom she recognized from court, tinkered with a green-and-yellow tractor.

"You make them work on a Sunday?"

He cocked an eyebrow. "Some of them ask to work Sundays to get through their service faster. Others have jobs during the week, so weekends are their community service time."

She cleared her throat. "Right."

"And you promised to take an objective look," Ethan said smoothly.

"I will."

A twist of his mouth conveyed his doubt. "Summer is our slowest time of year. We've finished calving, the cows are in summer pasture. The next couple of months are all about mending fences, maintaining machinery and putting up hay. Today, the guys are servicing the tractor."

"You know how to do that?" Cynthia asked the youths, who'd taken this excuse to lay down their tools.

"Getting there," one of them said.

"The good thing about a job like this," Ethan said, "is the guys who know something about cars get to practice their skills. Those who don't, pick up something new they can use immediately at home."

"This funnel is useless." Connor King, the nineteen-year-old she'd sentenced a couple of days ago, held up the offending piece of equipment. "It's taking forever to top up this stuff." He kicked at a pail labeled Transmission Oil.

"Careful," Ethan said. "You'll spill—"

The pail tipped over and viscous brown liquid glugged onto the concrete floor. The boy swore; Ethan jumped forward and righted the container.

He said slowly, "That's a five-gallon pail, Connor. A hundred and fifty dollars' worth. I reckon you just threw half of it away."

"Sorry," the kid muttered.

"No problem," Ethan said. "You can clean up the mess, then either you pay me back, or you work an extra six hours to cover the cost."

"No way, man." Connor's face turned scarlet. "You can't make me."

"I don't need to make you. You know the right thing to do." Ethan stared him down, arms folded.

For a tense twenty seconds—to Cynthia it felt like twenty minutes—no one spoke. Then

Connor broke away from Ethan. "Fine, I'll do the extra time. It's not as if there's anything else to do around here." He let out a string of curses, each cruder than the last.

Ethan's jaw locked. Cynthia watched him consciously relax his facial muscles before he said very quietly, "Apologize for your language."

Again, it seemed to take forever. Then Connor muttered, "Sorry, ma'am."

Cynthia exhaled noisily as Ethan moved on to show the boys how to change the brake fluid amid much kidding and bantering, which the kids evidently appreciated. When he judged the boys could be left to get on with the job, he steered her out of the barn.

They strolled to a paddock with a white rail fence that suggested it held horses rather than cows. Cynthia leaned against the rail. "Do you get many incidents like that?"

His eyebrows drew together. "That was nothing. These guys usually start here with a grudge against the world. Being willing to accept some accountability by the time they leave is the minimum I expect them to get out of the program. Though of course some get a lot further along."

"You handled Connor well."

"That's gracious of you." Ethan sounded as

if he didn't believe she meant it. He whistled to a horse she hadn't seen grazing over the far side. The chestnut animal abandoned its meal, trotted over.

"It's my objective opinion," she said, reminding him she was playing her part. "How did you manage not to lose your temper? I was ready to slug him."

"It's tempting, but of course it's not the answer." He fondled the horse's ears. The animal nickered and nudged closer. "I like Connor. I like all the kids who come here."

"Really? Because I struggle to like a lot of the people who come through my courtroom."

His mouth quirked. "By the time they get to me, you've knocked the fight out of them."

Connor had looked as though he still had plenty of fight.

"You asked me on Friday night—" Ethan's gaze drifted to her lips and she found herself pressing them together, minimizing them "—to give you a second chance. That's what these guys need, and a lot of them come into their own out here. Not so surprising I like them and they end up liking me."

A second chance. The reason she was in Stonewall Hollow. Because she'd messed up.

Though she hadn't broken any rules, other than her father's cardinal commandment: Thou shalt not let me down. "That's admirable," she said.

He scratched the horse's neck. "Does that mean Sam can serve out the rest of his sentence on the ranch?"

She should have seen that coming. "I haven't finished my assessment."

"Sam rides Stargirl." He patted the mare's neck. "He'd never been on horseback before, but he has a natural seat." A father's pride behind the throwaway comment. "Do you ride?"

"No. I don't wrangle cows, either," she admitted in a moment of…what? Wanting him to know the real her, limitations and all? The Cynthia her father couldn't accept? Ethan had made it clear he was well aware of her faults.

"And yet you think you can fit in around here?" But he didn't sound as if he was dismissing her.

"What do you think?" she challenged him.

"I'm still wondering why you want to. This isn't your kind of place."

She clamped her mouth shut, wanting to argue, knowing she didn't have much of a case. "Tell me more about your program. The administrative side."

"You mean the money." His cool tone matched hers.

"Hey, Ethan!" Connor called. "Where do I tip all this oil?"

"Jacob will show you!" Ethan yelled back. "Connor and Jacob used to throw punches at each other in high school. Out here, they pull together—when I force them to."

Impressive…but now she'd recalled her purpose, she wasn't about to be diverted. "So, the money?"

"Let's walk." He slapped the horse's rump and sent the animal on its way. "There's a trough over by the shelter belt—" he indicated a stand of pine trees beyond a wire fence "—that's been losing water. I patched it yesterday, I should check if it's holding."

He opened a gate that she suspected he'd normally climb over, and they started across the paddock. As they walked he explained the entire work program setup to her, patiently articulate. Cynthia made some mental calculations and figured that if today's shenanigans were anything to go by, the money he was paid to run the program didn't come near the hassle factor.

They reached the trough, which was half-full. Ethan hunkered down and stuck his arm in the cloudy water, feeling for his repair. "Seems okay. I'll check the level again tomorrow."

"Why do you help these kids?" Cynthia asked.

"To exploit the free labor." He dried his hands against his jeans.

"When we met, you told me you had a wild youth."

"Uh-huh."

Bending, Cynthia trailed a finger across the top of the water and watched the ripple that fanned out behind. "How wild?"

Ethan bit down on a *Butt out.* His past was none of her business and he wasn't about to tell her a damn thing. Amazing a woman could look so cute while she jabbed a guy with questions in all his most vulnerable places. Cynthia looked about eighteen in her tank top and cropped pants. Except her curves were more womanly. She shaded her eyes with her hand as she waited for his answer, and the pose lifted her breasts.

"Ethan?" she persisted.

He did what men had been doing since caveman times. Changed the subject.

"The problem with the kids who come

through the courts is often a lack of a decent male role model."

"If you don't want to tell me how wild you were, I'll ask the sheriff."

Of course, women had been ignoring men's attempts to change the subject since caveman times.

"Ask away," he said. The sheriff knew only what Ethan had told him.

"Strange that you're so good with the youths in your program, yet you struggle with Sam."

"Sam and I just need more time," he growled.

"Did you have a good male role model in your life? Your father?"

"This is not about me." He stabbed a finger at her. "Are you checking my qualifications to be Sam's dad? Because as far as I know, you're even less qualified to be a social worker than you are a judge. And I bet you don't know squat about families who don't fit the Atlanta mold. What's the bet you were born and raised in Buckhead—" the fanciest part of Atlanta "—and no one in your family ever got arrested?"

From the flicker in her eyes, he saw he was right. But being Cynthia, she came back fighting.

"My parents separated when I was three, and divorced on my fifth birthday, just in time for Dad to marry his second wife, who was pregnant with my youngest sister." She checked off each point on the fingers of her left hand. "Mom and Dad played bitter custody games for a few years, until Mom died of an aneurysm when I was ten."

Hell. "I'm sorry," he said.

She'd run out of fingers, but she kept going. "My stepmother, a wonderful woman, was killed in a car accident when I was twenty-one. My youngest sister couldn't walk for a year and a half after the crash." She was breathing hard, remembering.

"You poor kid."

She blinked. "I wasn't in the accident."

"I shouldn't have presumed to know anything about your life."

Her breathing slowed. "You're telling me I shouldn't about yours, either."

He shrugged.

"You asked me to reconsider Sam's sentence. I'm trying to understand what's best for him."

"I've told you what's best for him. I'm his father, I know him a hell of a lot better than you do."

"Fathers don't know everything," she said.

Was that hurt in her gray eyes? "Sounds like your dad put his kids through a lot, one way or another."

"My father is a wonderful man," she snapped. He'd forgotten she hated sympathy. "At least he's always been there for me."

"You think I've only known Sam three months by choice?" he demanded.

"Give me a reason why Sam should spend time here now that it suits you. One that's good for Sam."

He tipped his head back and stared at the cloudless sky.

"I dated Susan, Sam's mother, when I was eighteen. We broke up and I left town before either of us knew she was pregnant. She never told me about Sam."

Cynthia's mouth opened, then closed again as she processed the information. "Did your family know?"

He started walking back to the barn. She fell in beside him. "It was only me and my mom by then. She left town—we lived in Augusta—soon after I did, so she didn't know about the baby, either."

"What if Susan had told you she was pregnant?"

The big question he'd never get a chance to answer. Ethan stopped in the middle of the paddock. Cynthia did, too. "Hell, I was pretty angry at life back then," he said. "But I like to think I'd have stepped up to the plate. It might even have prevented me doing some stupid things."

She nodded, though she could have no idea what he meant. "So how did Sam know where to find you?"

"His mom kept tabs on me, in case Sam needed me for medical reasons or whatever. When she ran out of patience with his antics, she sent him here in the hope I could handle him." Susan's exact words were *Your genes made him like this, you deal with him.*

"It must have been a shock," Cynthia said, "to discover you had a son."

"That doesn't begin to describe it." He fixed his gaze on the horizon. "I was furious with Susan for not telling me sooner. But I understood."

She scuffed the grass with her sneaker. It was still green, but another month or so of these temperatures would surely burn it off. By then, he and the boys would have all the hay in. With or without Sam's help.

"It sounds inexcusable," she said.

Yeah, the judge saw everything in black and white. Ethan wondered how little he could get away with telling her. Because the truth would have her labeling him an unfit parent. "Susan didn't think I'd be good for Sam."

So far, she was proving right, though not for the reasons she'd thought. Ironic that other kids' parents thanked him for his help, but when it came to his own son…

"Do you like him?" Cynthia asked.

Air flew out of his lungs. "What kind of question is that?"

"He's almost a stranger," she observed. "I assume you love him at some elemental level, because he's your son."

"Of course I do." He lengthened his stride. "Your visit to the Double T is about making a decision on the facts. Being the judge doesn't give you the right to pry into my personal life."

"You said you like all the kids in your program. You don't have to spend time with them, but you do. Is Sam someone you'd choose to spend time with?"

"Damn straight he is." He pounced on the question. "You're the one who's preventing me doing just that."

The hint of a breeze sent a strand of blond

hair drifting across her face. "You have evenings together, don't you?"

For Sam's sake, Ethan answered. "There's something about the evenings that doesn't work. We're both tired, and with just the two of us, no one else to take the heat, it's too easy for disagreements to escalate. He thinks I'm always on his case, but it's not how it is."

"Does he know how much you care about him? It's easy for kids to doubt their parents."

He frowned. "I'm not good at telling him how I feel, but I do my best to show him. Sam likes the ranch—he tries to hide it but I can see. Having him work here during the day would let us focus on something that's potentially important to both of us."

Something sparked in her eyes. Had something he said resonated with her? Ethan held his breath. Her lips parted, then closed again, her head tilted appraisingly. "If Sam didn't like the ranch, would that change the way you feel about him?"

He had the feeling this was the sixty-four-thousand-dollar question, though he couldn't think why. "I love my son. I loved him the moment Susan called and told me he existed and he was on his way here. That will never change."

What he didn't love was the way the feeling had sprung up so instantly, so intense. Beyond his control.

"The troubles you're having," she said tentatively, "they don't make you love him less?"

"I guess love isn't about what someone does or doesn't do," he said to the sky. "It's about who they are in your life." As if he was any kind of expert. But if he was only going to love Sam for good behavior, he'd have given up by now.

Still, Cynthia seemed to be waiting. Dammit, what else did he have to give? Her expression had softened. That had to be good, right?

"You asked…if I like Sam." Getting each word out was like sneezing stones. "I don't know him. I want… I really want to know him and to like him."

She let out a little sigh. "Thank you." She smiled. It turned her eyes a silvery color, made her mouth temptingly mobile.

"You're welcome, though I have no idea for what." Though answering her questions had drained him, Ethan smiled back and there was that *zing* that shouldn't still be taking him by surprise with her.

A knot loosened between his shoulder blades. Over beyond the barn, tires crunched on gravel, too fast, skidding. But it didn't put his hackles up the way it usually did. "That'll be Sam now."

He realized he was pleased his son was back. And relieved—even more relieved than he'd been when Sam left.

The electric-blue Mazda came into sight. The driver's window was open and Ethan lifted a hand in greeting. As he got a few steps closer, he cursed before he could stop himself.

"What's wrong?" Cynthia scrambled to catch up.

Neutral voice. "Sam's brought my mom. I wasn't expecting her." He'd all but persuaded Cynthia that Sam's place was here with him. What were the chances he could hold everything together now?

"Your mother lives in Stonewall Hollow?"

"She moved here soon after I did. She has a place in town." He cursed again, this time keeping it inside. Things were about to get weird. He should have told Cynthia earlier who his mom was.

Chapter Eight

Ethan watched Cynthia tug down her tank and pat her hair into place. As if she was a teenager about to meet her boyfriend's parents. He had the crazy thought she was the kind of girl a guy would be proud to bring home to his mom.

Not him. Not his mom.

The passenger door opened, and his mother climbed out. Ethan tried to see her the way Cynthia would, minus the baggage. A short, slim woman, looking good for her fifty-three years. She'd easily pass for mid-forties. Casually dressed in inexpensive jeans and a T-shirt, with open-toed sandals that he knew without seeing would reveal red nail polish. She looked like a normal mom.

"Afternoon," she called. Then she saw Cynthia. "Oh, you have company." She glanced at Sam, who shrugged.

Cynthia grabbed Ethan's arm, her fingers heating his skin where they wrapped around him. "*Your mom* is the mayor's assistant? Why didn't you say so when I mentioned her the other night?"

"We were talking about you coming out to the ranch. I was in the middle of a poker game. It wasn't relevant." Three excuses, each as spurious as the last.

"Was it *relevant* when we were talking about your past just now?" She released his arm as his mom reached them.

"Ethan." Linnet didn't kiss him. They weren't that kind of mother and son.

"Mom." If they were handing out awards for family interaction, he and his mother would win the booby prize. *Don't blow it.* "I believe you've met Cynthia Merritt, our new judge? Cynthia, this is my mom, Linnet Robinson."

The two women shook hands, both cool.

Sam returned Cynthia's greeting in a civilized manner that made his grandmother beam. She moved closer to him. “Sam invited me for supper.”

Of course he did, because he knew Ethan didn’t want her here today.

“I brought a salad,” Linnet said. “I hope I’m not in the way.”

Ethan forced a smile. “It’s fine.” Dammit, he should have told Cynthia about his mom. Now she would think they had some peculiar, dysfunctional relationship. Oh, yeah…

“I didn’t realize Ethan had family so close,” Cynthia said. “Close *by*,” she elaborated deliberately.

“How about we go inside?” he suggested, an attempt at normalcy he knew was doomed to fail. But he had to try. “Janet—my housekeeper,” he explained to Cynthia, “left tea in the fridge.”

Her jerky nod said she still wanted to know why he hadn’t told her Linnet was his mom. He led the way into the open plan living and dining room that ran the entire front of the long house. The dining room backed onto the kitchen, and behind the living room was the den he used as his office.

“This room is amazing.” Cynthia wandered over to look at the red-and-white rag rug that hung above the mantelpiece. She sounded surprised, as if she'd expected his home to be as much of a mess as his relationship with Sam. "Did you decorate it yourself?"

"It's pretty much as the previous owners had it." Ethan loved the house, simple and sprawling though it was. "I painted a few walls, had some couches reupholstered. It works for me."

Linnet sat down at the pine dining table. Cynthia pulled out a chair, too.

"Can I pour you some tea, Gram?" Sam offered.

"Thanks, honey."

Ethan had to be some kind of monster, to resent his mom looking at Sam with that tender warmth.

Typically, as soon as Sam had offered the tea, he forgot about it. He sat down with the two women. Ethan would have reminded him, but he didn't need Sam getting uncooperative in front of Cynthia.

As he pulled glasses from the cupboard, he heard Linnet answering a question from Cynthia. "I've been here eleven years. I arrived about a year after Ethan."

He froze…then moved to get the tea from the fridge. His mom wouldn't blab the full, grim truth about his past. They'd agreed it was best for Sam not to know—it was about the only thing they did agree on.

He inadvertently banged his mother's glass down on the table, drawing a curious glance from Cynthia.

"Thanks." Linnet added an extra spoon of sugar to the already sweet tea and stirred.

He set another glass in front of Sam, with little expectation he would drink it. Sam didn't seem to want anything from Ethan. If it wasn't for hunger pangs, Ethan doubted the kid would even eat.

"Are you doing the late shift at Al's tonight?" he asked. It would explain why Sam had brought Linnet out in his car; he could take her home on his way to work.

"Yeah, sole charge. Al says he trusts me more than his own son." There was a challenge in Sam's eyes that Ethan wasn't about to meet in front of his mom and Cynthia.

"Great," he said, his lower face stiff.

Linnet wanted to slap Ethan's cheeks until he snapped out of the calm and responsible manner he considered good parenting. But her son would never take advice from her, even if she got up the guts to offer it.

It was easier to deal with Sam, even when

he scowled. The sullenness disguised his good looks, but Linnet saw past that. She patted the back of his hand. “Don’t mind your dad, he’s been wearing that poker face longer than I can remember.” It had frustrated the heck out of her in the days when she’d wanted Ethan to pretend, to make an effort, even a tiny one, for the sake of harmony in their home.

At a glance from Ethan, she realized she’d done it again. Hurt him in her attempt to placate. She should fix it. But she knew the words would come out wrong. She gave up too easily, of course, always had.

Which was why, although she’d moved to Stonewall Hollow specifically to get close to Ethan, she’d barely progressed in eleven years. She’d make an effort, be rebuffed, give up. Then find herself, out of hurt, rejecting Ethan’s rare, halfhearted attempts at reconciliation. By the time her skin thickened and she was ready to try again, Ethan would have lost interest.

She had no trouble identifying the pattern. Changing it was the problem.

“Sam’s a hard worker,” Ethan was telling the judge. The compliment didn’t lessen Sam’s ferocious expression. “He’ll turn his hand to pretty much anything.”

Linnet recognized a quality in his voice when he spoke to the judge that she hadn't heard in a long time. A softening, barely discernible, but it made her catch her breath. Was Ethan attracted to Cynthia? After what she'd done, refusing his request to have Sam work with him?

Linnet wasn't a hundred percent sure if Sam should be working on the ranch, but she could tell how upset Ethan had been. Cynthia Merritt didn't have any right to turn him down, not after the good work he did with those kids. And Ethan had it in him to be a better parent than Linnet had ever been.

"How long are you in town, Judge Merritt?" she asked.

Cynthia sipped her tea. "I'm not sure. It's a temporary position, as you know."

"Must have been difficult, leaving your family," Linnet said.

"Mm-hmm."

Linnet wondered if she liked Ethan back. She seemed cold, reserved. Ethan needed a woman who would support him and put him first.

She forced a friendly smile. "Did you leave a boyfriend in Atlanta?" Good grief, where had she found the courage to ask that? Ethan was gaping, and the judge looked as if she wanted to incarcerate her. Linnet gritted her teeth and held her smile.

"No."

Pity. "My son is single, too, but never for long," Linnet informed her. "He dates a lot of women." It was true, though he never dated seriously enough to break hearts.

"How interesting," Cynthia said frostily. But there was an infinitesimal adjustment in her posture, away from Ethan.

"Which reminds me—" shaking at her own temerity, Linnet resolutely ignored Ethan's glare and dived for a change of subject "—well done on sending Paul Dayton to jail."

"That's not what you told the reporter."

If the judge had been more cooperative with Ethan, Linnet might have been nicer about her to Tania. She stirred her tea and decided to ignore Cynthia's comment. "Believe me, I know what it's like to marry a deadbeat like Dayton. I just hope Kathy sees sense and leaves him. Otherwise her kids will never forgive her."

Why didn't she just take off both shoes and stuff her feet into her mouth?

"You did what you thought best, Mom," Ethan said tautly.

As if he believed that.

"Gram, it's not your fault you and him—" Sam jerked his head toward Ethan "—don't get along."

There were so many things wrong with that statement, Ethan didn't know where to start. "You and *he*." He chose to tackle his son's grammar, the least of them.

Linnet rolled her eyes, as if she knew a whole lot about raising a decent kid. The familiar taste of unresolved bitterness filled his mouth.

"Are you entering any of the contests at the county fair, Sam?" Cynthia asked.

"We're both on the Confederate team in the tug of war," Ethan told her.

Sam fished a slice of lemon out of his tea with his finger. "And I'm entering the rodeo."

"You're not entering the rodeo," Ethan said.

Sam sucked the lemon and didn't reply. He took after his grandma, refusing to engage when it didn't suit him. How was Ethan supposed to reason with him? What would he say to one of the kids on his work program?

"You're a good rider, Sam—" encouragement first "—but you don't have enough experience to ride in the rodeo, it's too dangerous. Next year, though, you'll be right on it." Bad news second, neatly sugarcoated.

The twist of Sam's mouth suggested he'd bitten right through the sugarcoating. "I want to ride. Dean's dad said I'm good enough."

Dean's dad, Dean's dad. Anyone would think Sam was eight, not eighteen, the rate at which his friend's father came up in a whine. "Dean's dad lost the sensible part of his brain in a rodeo accident twenty years ago."

"What's your horse's name?" Cynthia asked.

Sam gave her an incredulous look. Linnet tittered.

It was the second time in as many minutes Cynthia had deflected the tension between Ethan and Sam. Did she realize Sam was making trouble in her honor?

"I guess you're too old for that kind of question," Cynthia apologized. "Where do you like to ride—I've seen signs to various paths and trails around town."

Amazingly, that did capture Sam's attention. He talked about a couple of the trails near the ranch and the challenges and sights they presented. "I saw a bald eagle the other day," he concluded, unable to contain his enthusiasm.

"Wonderful," Cynthia said.

Sam managed to look simultaneously pleased and resentful.

"Al told me this morning you're doing a great job at the gas station," Ethan said.

"Yeah?" Sam eyed him expectantly. Expecting what? For the millionth time, Ethan felt as if he'd stepped out of his depth. He never had this trouble with the kids on the ranch.

"You did a good job with the hay, too," he said. "At home."

Sam nodded, still waiting.

"You could probably show Connor and Jacob a thing or two about getting those bales tight."

"Sure." Sam dripped sarcasm. He stood, made a halfhearted effort to hoist up his too low-riding jeans. "Thanks for the tea."

Ethan wondered what he'd failed to say. "I'd appreciate if you could help the guys finish up with the tractor."

"I take it that's an order."

"Correct." Ethan sounded more starched than a tuxedo shirt.

Sam stomped outside, tea untouched. Through the window, Ethan watched his loose stride, at odds with the set of his shoulders. He chanced a glance at Cynthia, whose expression was carefully blank. Yep, she was thinking his family was out of control.

She was right.

"How's the boy supposed to feel as if you're his dad, when you're always barking orders at him?" Linnet asked.

"As opposed to your supportive parenting style?" Dammit, how had that slipped out?

Linnet's face took on a tomato hue, her hands flapped at her sides. "I have no idea what you're talking about."

Ethan mouthed the words as she said them. He'd chisel that phrase on his mother's gravestone one day.

Cynthia drained her glass and stood. "I need to go." She was looking at him as if he was the playground bully.

Ethan escorted her out to her Volvo.

"The history between me and Mom is complicated," he said as they crossed the sunbaked dirt. "But we don't see a lot of each other, so she doesn't have any effect on my work program."

Cynthia pressed the remote to unlock the car. Only a city girl would lock it out here. "She has a relationship with Sam."

He opened her door. "It's good for him to get along with his grandmother." In theory.

She paused halfway into the car, her right hand curled over the top of the door. "Ethan, your work program is very impressive. I'll have no reservations about sending kids to you."

Before he could think, he grabbed her other hand. "That's fantastic." He ran his thumb over her knuckles down to her tapered fingertips. If he laced her fingers through his…

"About Sam," she said. "I know he was laying it on for my benefit today, but that doesn't change the underlying truth. He's not going to cooperate with you the way things are now. And when you could be using your mom as an ally, you won't because you don't get along with her. Not all your fault, I'm sure, but that's the way it is."

Ethan's chest constricted; he dropped her hand. "You're not reassigning Sam?"

She slid into her seat and turned the key in the ignition. The engine purred. "I'm sorry, Ethan, but Sam stays where he is."

She made to close the door, but he grabbed it. "You conned me. You had me answer all those personal questions thinking it would help. Instead, you're using it to keep Sam away." He'd hated answering those questions, yet by the end it had felt cathartic. All along, she'd been stitching him up.

"*You* conned *me,*" she retorted. "When we talked in the paddock, you made it sound as if you'd do whatever it took to make things work with Sam. But you can't even hold a polite conversation with his grandmother."

"So that's it, end of story?" He thumped the roof of the car. "I ought to go ahead and lodge that complaint about you."

Her eyes widened. "You promised not to."

"I wasn't under oath."

"You're a man of your word."

He growled.

She buzzed down her window, then pulled the door shut. "That goes for the other part of our deal, too."

"You can't seriously think—"

"I kept my side," she said. "I took an objective look at this place, and I gave you sound reasons for my decision. Now you need to do your bit. To convince people in this town that you like me and they should, too."

It wasn't until her car had almost rounded the bend in the drive, spitting dust in its wake, that the solution to her unreasonableness hit Ethan. She wasn't the only one who could set a person up for a fall.

"Brilliant," he muttered with grim satisfaction as he turned back to the house and the prospect of dinner with his mother and son.

He would keep his promise to Cynthia, all right. And at the same time drive her out of town.

Two weeks, max, and she'd be gone, or he'd eat his best Stetson.

Cynthia was munching a tuna sandwich at her desk during Monday's noon recess when Ethan walked into her chambers.

Hard on the heels of her irritation at his failure to knock came an unbidden *Mmm, he looks great in that black T-shirt.* That's what you got when you let a handsome but bad-tempered rancher hold your hand, even just for a minute. She swallowed her appreciation along with her mouthful.

"Hi," she said cautiously. She hadn't expected to see him so soon; he'd been understandably mad when she left yesterday.

"I'm here to keep my end of the deal." The words were not quite a snarl.

"Really?" She rewrapped the remains of her sandwich. "Because if that scowl is your I-like-the-judge face, it needs work." She'd had no choice but to refuse to send Sam to the Double T. His relationship with his father was too fragile to take much more pressure. She just wished she didn't feel so bad for Ethan. Those things he'd said about his feelings for Sam…he'd meant them, in his own way.

His scowl deepened as he set his hat on her desk. "In public," he said. "That's when I need to act as if I like you. So let's go."

"Go where?" She put the sandwich in her drawer. She'd been thinking about how he could help boost her image, and she had a couple of ideas. She didn't imagine he'd been thinking along the same lines.

"We're due to meet with Jackson Bream in five minutes," Ethan said. "He's the head of the Griffin County Fair organizing committee. And your new best friend."

According to the dozens of posters around town, the fair would open this Friday night, running through the weekend—Sunday was the Fourth—to wrap up on Tuesday.

"Why is he my friend?" Cynthia asked.

"The fair is the number one event on Stonewall Hollow's annual calendar, and Jackson can make you the star."

She pushed back from her desk. "I'm not entering any kind of pageant." There was only one star in the Merritt family, and that was Sabrina.

"Not a pageant," he said. "What I have in mind is perfect for you."

"Why are you being so helpful?" she demanded. "You're mad at me."

His eyes flickered. "We have an agreement. Now, let's get over to Jackson's office. You need to be back for afternoon court."

"They can't start without me," she said tartly, borrowing Melanie's truism as she followed him out of her chambers.

They walked across the square and down Green Street, a road she had yet to explore. A couple of people greeted Ethan as they passed.

"We're in public," Cynthia pointed out the second time he failed to introduce her. "Could you act a little friendlier toward me?"

He bared his teeth in a ferocious smile. "Better?"

"Much," she lied.

"Too bad we're already there so no one else will get to see our wonderful rapport." He pointed to the upper story of an art deco–style building across the street. Bright pink lettering said Miss Honey's Dancers. "Jackson works out of an office above Miss Honey's."

"Above a *brothel?*" Cynthia asked.

"I've never met anyone as suspicious as you." Ethan grabbed her elbow as they stepped off the curb. "Miss Honey's is a dance school. For kids."

The fair's headquarters was a rabbit warren of offices, each smaller and darker than the last. But after they'd walked through three rooms, with Ethan greeting various administrative staff en route—painstakingly introducing Cynthia each time—the space opened out into a large, low-ceiling office.

Framed photographs and news clippings from past fairs crammed the walls. Beneath the window, a glass-fronted sideboard held an array of ribbons, rosettes and silver cups. In the center of the room, a man who reminded Cynthia of those portraits of Civil War generals—right down to the craggy eyebrows, thick mustache and full beard—presided over a chipped Formica desk.

"Granger." He barked the name, military-style. Cynthia managed not to salute.

"Hey, Jackson." In contrast, Ethan's greeting was a slow meander. "May I introduce Judge Cynthia Merritt?"

Jackson Bream came around the desk to clasp her hand in both his. "Your Honor."

"Cynthia, please," she urged.

He fingered the end of his mustache. "Ethan

tells me you want to help out with our little fair."

She gathered from Ethan's significant look that she wasn't supposed to let the man get away with denigrating his own fair.

"I hear it's the biggest event this side of Disneyworld," she said.

And caught a smothered laugh from Ethan. She started to relax.

Jackson wagged a finger at her. "Not at all, my dear, as I'm sure you know." He sounded pleased, just the same. "What we do has nothing on some of the bigger fairs around the state, but we put on an impressive show for the size of the county, and each year a local charity benefits to a measurable extent."

"I can't wait to get involved," Cynthia said.

Muted music wafted up from the dance studio below. A strong, rhythmic beat accompanied by soft thumps, the pitter-patter of not-so-tiny feet. The kids must be learning hip-hop.

"When Ethan told me how keen you are to help out, I was thrilled," Jackson said. "You don't know how hard it is—"

"Why don't you explain what Cynthia will be doing?" Ethan interrupted.

Jackson pulled a sheet of paper from the

top drawer of his desk. "I printed off a list of the fair's amateur contests, in anticipation."

Cynthia scanned the list. Cakes, Cookies, Pies, Preserved Food. Then Bonsai, Children's Art, Giant Onion…and on it went. She felt a frown line forming between her eyes. "You want me to enter all of these?"

Jackson laughed. "Certainly not. You can't enter, not if you're the judge."

It took her a moment to understand. "You want me to judge bonsai? And preserves?"

"Anyone can pickle an onion or grow a half-assed tree, but not everyone can judge," Ethan said. "Take a look at the photos around the walls."

Cynthia stood and went to peruse some of the pictures. Most of them were framed newspaper clippings. More than half featured the contest judge congratulating a beribboned winner. Smiles all around. A lightbulb went off in her head. "This is perfect," she told Ethan excitedly.

He spread his hands to say, *I told you so.*

"I mean, I'm not an expert cook, but how hard can it be to taste a few cakes and hand out trophies?"

"Ah," Jackson said. "I should point out—"

"Exactly," Ethan said.

She turned to Jackson. "I'll do it. Please."

"Wonderful." The older man saluted her. "So I have you down for craft contests, plus the baby pageant?"

"Babies?" Cynthia glanced at the photo on the wall of an extremely round baby being cuddled by a previous judge. "I don't know…"

"They're a highlight of the fair," Ethan encouraged her.

She shrugged. "Okay, what the heck. I judge every other age group in court, I might as well move down to babies."

"I'm in your debt," Jackson said. Grandly, he added, "All of Stonewall Hollow is in your debt." He kissed her cheek.

They agreed on a starting time for judging on Saturday, then Ethan reminded Cynthia it was time to get back to court.

"I really appreciate what you did there," Cynthia said as they crossed the square. "It was more than generous of you."

"You agreed to keep sending kids to the ranch." His loping stride had her almost jogging to keep up. She hitched her skirt above her knees so she could lengthen her steps. Ethan glanced down at her legs, then fixed his gaze straight ahead.

"I feel bad that I couldn't do more for you and Sam," she admitted.

If possible, he walked faster. "That's over with."

They reached the white wooden gazebo that marked the center of the square.

"Can we stop a moment?" Panting, Cynthia clutched the green-topped rail that ran around the open sides of the gazebo and caught her breath. Saturday's run hadn't done much to improve her fitness.

Ethan halted a few yards ahead of her. He scanned the grassy area, the benches where people ate sandwiches in the sunshine, the paved pathways, and beyond, the fanciful facade of the courthouse.

"I know you don't like me, despite the glowing account you gave Jackson," she said.

He swiveled to check the clock tower above city hall, then glanced at his watch.

"But I'm wondering if you could help me some more."

"What?" He closed the gap between them, loomed over her.

"The fair is great," she said quickly. "But Tania, the reporter, is already questioning people about me—she spoke to Melanie's sister. I thought maybe if you and I had lunch together, say, tomorrow…"

"No way," he said. "It won't take five minutes for the news you're judging at the fair to get around, and everyone will know what a great gal you are. You don't need me."

"I just think it would help—"

He leaned in close, and she saw white tension in the lines around his mouth. "I've given you every chance to do the right thing for my son."

"Which is exactly what I've done," she said.

"I said nice things about you to Jackson and got you a job at the fair, it's up to you to make what you can of it. There's no reason for you and me to have anything more to do with each other."

"In court—"

"Sure, I'll see you in court, where I expect you to keep your word and send some of those kids out to the ranch. But that's business. On a personal level, I've done everything I'm going to do for you. Ever. Get it?"

The sun beat down on Cynthia's temples, frying her brain. There was no other explanation for why the distance in Ethan's voice should feel like a slap in the face. Like he was throwing her out of his life, the way her dad had thrown her out of Atlanta. She'd never been *in* his life, not beyond a brief, scorching kiss. And a conversation that had held more honesty, more meaning, than any other she could remember.

"I get it," she said through tight lips.

With a tip of his hat, Ethan walked away.

Chapter Nine

By Wednesday morning, any vestige of hurt at Ethan's behavior had been replaced by good, old-fashioned rage. Barely able to think straight, let alone deal out justice, Cynthia declared an early recess in court and called Ethan's cell phone at eleven-thirty.

"You *jerk,*" she said. It felt great. "You *double-dealing* jerk." Even better. Shame she couldn't vent like this in Atlanta.

"Is this about a court case, Judge Merritt?"

"You bet—my imminent trial for your murder."

"That sounds personal," he said. "And now

that I've set you up with the best job in town, you and I don't do personal."

"You set me up all right," she retorted. "You need to *un*-set me. Your housekeeper told me you're in town, can we meet?"

"No can do." Fake regret. "I have a lunch engagement."

She was dodging bullets all over town, and he had a date? "That's not good enough."

"That's all you're going to get." Silence. She was listening to dead air.

When she hung up, the phone rang immediately. She grabbed it. "Ethan?"

"Judge Merritt, this is Tania Leach from the *Gazette.* I have a couple more questions to follow up our interview."

I bet you do. She shuddered. "Tania, I'm sorry, I'll need to call you back."

"When?" the woman asked.

"Uh..." *Never.* "Later."

As soon as she'd got rid of the woman, Cynthia grabbed her dusky pink suit jacket from the back of her chair and headed out of her chambers. There weren't that many places to meet someone for lunch in Stonewall Hollow. She would find Ethan and make him help her.

She hit pay dirt at Sally's Diner, the second

restaurant she visited. She marched up to the booth where Ethan sat, and plunked herself opposite him.

He didn't seem surprised. Just lifted a finger to attract the attention of Evie, Sally's daughter, and called out, "Another slice of the loganberry pie, for the judge, please, Evie."

"Just a coffee, no pie for me," Cynthia said through gritted teeth.

"How about a tiny piece?" Evie suggested with a wide smile, as Cynthia had known she would. "I know Mom would like you to try it." She hurried toward the kitchen.

"I forgot to ask if you want ice cream with your pie," Ethan said.

"You forgot to tell me that judging at the county fair would wreck my life."

"I hear court's going well this week."

"Smoother than a leg wax," she agreed. The mention of female beauty procedures didn't jolt him out of his indifference. At least, not in the way she wanted. She detected a stifled laugh.

"That's great," he said. "I heard your public approval is off the scale."

He was right, and she was taking shameless advantage of everyone being on their best behavior. She'd been able to report positively to her father, who was apparently dropping words in all the right ears about the judge job. His support warmed her, it felt almost like old, pre–broom closet times. But right now, that wasn't the point.

"You wouldn't believe how many people have dropped a cake or cookies around to my place this week—" she made quote marks with her fingers "—just to say welcome." She sat back. "Or rather, you would believe it, I'm sure."

"The locals can be friendly," he agreed.

"Beth somebody brought me a pound cake. Mrs. Baker, the head of the local chapter of Daughters of the American Revolution, brought a pineapple upside-down cake. To name just two."

"Sounds delicious. Though you might need to start watching your weight." He conducted a blatant scrutiny of her face, her neck, the V of her pale gray silk wrap top, then leaned forward. "On second thought, I don't think you need to worry."

She leaned forward, too. "Didn't you say you and I were past personal talk?"

"A momentary lapse. I apologize."

"You know very well I'm going to taste all those items again in the contest," she hissed.

"Don't tell me this—this revenge plan of yours isn't personal."

Evie returned with two coffees. She set a piece of loganberry pie in front of Cynthia. Then the same for Ethan, with ice cream.

"That's the thing you don't yet understand about small towns. Everything's personal." He spooned up half his ice cream and deposited it on her slice of pie. "When you see that distinctive pineapple upside-down cake, or that familiar pound cake frosting, you'll remember the kind person who brought it to you…."

"Admit it, you did this deliberately."

"You wanted to get to know the town—this is what we're like."

Cynthia bent her head over her pie. She'd realized he'd set her up, but not expected him to acknowledge it. Her eyes stung. So that's where Sam got his honesty. Stalling for time before she'd have to look at Ethan, she dug her fork into the pie she hadn't intended to eat and took a bite.

It was too hot—she fanned her mouth.

"Everyone is desperate to win the contests," she said, when she was certain her voice would be steady.

"Yep." He stared hard at her and she drew

on her deepest reserves of calm. "People don't take losing too well, either."

He didn't give a damn about her.

"My sister judged a giant pumpkin contest once," Cynthia said. "Sabrina received a death threat."

He recoiled, then said, "I don't believe you."

"It's true." She didn't mention that the letter had come from an eighty-five-year-old woman suffering dementia.

"We don't have a giant pumpkin contest," he muttered.

"We have giant onions."

"No one's going to kill you over an onion."

"Like you'd care if they did." She pushed her plate away. "How have previous judges handled the problem of vengeful losers?"

He reached across and forked up some of her pie. "Usually, we get someone from out of town. They hightail it back where they came from the minute they've finished handing out the medals."

She drew in a sharp breath. "That's what this is about? Scaring me back to Atlanta?"

"You know you don't fit in here."

Pain stabbed behind her ribs. "Your little campaign won't work."

"Scaring you out of town would have been the icing on the cake, if you'll pardon the pun," he said. "But I already figured you have more guts than a prize heifer."

"Stop comparing me to your stupid cows," she ordered.

"Cows aren't as dumb as they seem." He took another bite of her pie. "And they have four stomachs. So they literally have a lot of guts."

She couldn't believe she was tempted to take his nonsense as a compliment. She scowled. "If you knew I wasn't going to run away, why did you set me up?"

"I figure a lot of those unhappy people after the fair will want to talk to Tania about that article in the *Gazette,* which for some reason is a big deal to you," he said. "Chances are, some of them might have been in court recently, or else their family members have. Their disappointment might even prompt them to lodge that complaint you conned me out of."

"I didn't con you—"

He tossed his fork into her plate; it clattered against the china. "Did you for one second seriously entertain the idea of having Sam work at the ranch?" he demanded.

"I…uh…" She fidgeted with the paper napkin in her lap.

"You made me tell you what I was thinking, what I was feeling, and all along it wouldn't make a blind bit of difference," he accused her. "You conned me."

"Okay, so I was *almost* sure before we started that Sam shouldn't work with you. But you've had your revenge—I haven't slept since Monday, and my blood pressure's probably off the scale. We're even. Help me get out of this judging without upsetting everyone."

"Not a chance," he said. "You can't leave a whole town in the lurch and not have it come back to bite you. At least if you do the judging, the winners will be happy and might say something nice about you to Tania—they'll counteract the losers. If you don't judge, no one's happy."

Cynthia pressed the heels of her hands into her eyes.

"Hey," Ethan protested.

"My family knows the *Gazette* is running an article about me," she said. "There's no way they won't see it."

"They're not going to believe some hick town newspaper."

She lowered her hands to the table. "Reputation is very important to my father—his and mine."

Ethan rubbed the back of his neck. "Just tell him you were set up."

"He doesn't like people with a victim mentality."

Ethan snorted.

"My sisters are both incredibly successful," she continued.

"So are you."

"And they both just got married." Oops, she hadn't planned to say that.

"Uh..." Ethan's glance around the café was slightly wild-eyed. "They're probably too busy to read the paper?"

That uncertainty in his voice was guilt, Cynthia realized. She was a judge, she was very familiar with guilt. And punishment. "They'll read it." She injected deep gloom into the words.

"You'll cope," Ethan said. "You're a fighter."

She let her shoulders droop. "I'm sick of fighting. Do you realize, a woman I'd never met gave me a bunch of welcome-to-our-town flowers the other day, and for one second I was so happy. I actually thought she might like me, might appreciate that I'd volunteered to judge at the fair."

"She probably did," Ethan said uncomfortably. "There's no flower arranging contest."

Cynthia gave a hollow laugh. "Then she mentioned her adorable daughter who always draws a fairy in the bottom righthand corner of her paintings."

Ethan picked up his fork in silence and used it to worry at her pie. "If you're that concerned, you could leave town before the fair. An urgent recall to the city."

"I can't leave," she said tightly. "Though right now I'd like nothing better."

He chewed the last mouthful of her pie, lost in thought. Sally, the diner's owner, approached their table.

"Could you smile at me, please?" Cynthia asked him.

"Huh?"

"Sally's coming. Please act as if you like me."

"Everything okay, folks?" Sally asked.

"The pie was delicious, wasn't it, Ethan?" Cynthia beamed at him.

For a moment, she thought he would show Sally just how little he thought of her. Then his face relaxed. He smiled. “It was great, *Cindy.*”

She didn’t react to the contraction of her name.

“Thanks, Judge,” Sally said. “When I make it at home, I use more vanilla,” she added significantly.

Ethan’s eyes met Cynthia’s.

Sally cleared their plates. “Sheriff said Judge Piet has taken a turn for the worse, did you all hear that?”

The sheriff hadn’t bothered to tell Cynthia, but she murmured agreement.

“Maybe we’ll have you with us a little longer,” Sally said brightly. “That’d be nice.”

Ethan snorted.

“Pie’s on the house,” Sally declared.

She couldn’t have played into Cynthia’s hands better if she’d tried. “Thanks, but I’ll pay my way. Wouldn’t want people to think I can be influenced at the fair.”

Ethan winced; Sally’s face reddened.

“I’m sure that’s not what you’re doing,” Cynthia added. “But some petty-minded people might choose to misinterpret your generosity.”

“There are plenty of small minds around,” Sally agreed. “Watch out for Helen Trainer—

she thinks her lattice tops are something else. Last year, she practically stalked the judge."

It was all Cynthia could do not to dance a jig on the table at Sally's confirmation of the danger Ethan had put her in.

"*Stalked* might be an exaggeration," Ethan said.

The moment Sally left, Cynthia said, "I need your help. Please."

He looked torn. Then he glanced past her. "Let's talk later."

Later might be too late. Ethan might have remembered his grudge against her by *later.* "The fair is only a couple of days away."

His expression shuttered. "You need to go." He stood.

What was that about? Cynthia twisted in her seat. And saw Linnet walking toward them. Ethan's lunch date was his mom?

"I'll pay the check," he assured her.

She picked up her cold coffee and took a slow, disinterested sip.

Ethan realized he was bracing himself for rejection, even though his mom had sounded pleased, if wary, when he'd called to suggest lunch. That bracing was something he unconsciously did every time he saw her. A learned behavior. He tried to dismiss the thought, which would surely lead to resentment.

It wasn't so difficult, since he had more on his mind than his mom. Did Cynthia really believe her family would think less of her because of a disparaging newspaper article?

"I didn't realize she was coming along." Linnet nodded at Cynthia.

Don't start, Mom. "Cynthia's just leaving."

"Actually, I just got here," Cynthia said.

Linnet took in the remains of Cynthia's pie, now on his side of the table. "You already ate."

She was always trying to read something into everything he did. She said it was because he would never say what he was thinking, but they both knew she didn't really want to hear his thoughts. "I've put in some hard work this morning," he said. "The pie was a snack while I waited."

At last she gave in and sat down. Next to Cynthia.

"Aren't you due back in court?" he asked the judge.

"Not until one-thirty." She smiled at him again, the "best buddies" smile she'd used with Sally. Did she really think his apparent goodwill would save her, come the fair on Saturday?

"I'm having the Reuben," he said to his mom, to forestall her curiosity.

Linnet perused the menu, which she must have known by heart. "I haven't tried the club sandwich in a while."

"Club sandwich it is," he said heartily.

"Green salad for me," Cynthia said.

"Mom and I have some things to discuss. Privately."

"Since," she continued as if he hadn't spoken, "green salad is about the only food I don't have to judge on Saturday." She gave him another smile, this one dazzling. Disconcertingly, his body tightened. With his mother right there.

"The trouble with judging at the fair is it's so easy to get it wrong if you're not a people person," Linnet said.

You could rely on her to dig like a miner on steroids. In his heart Ethan knew she couldn't help those comments, they came out of a deep-rooted insecurity. Didn't make them any less infuriating.

"Ethan thinks I'm a people person, don't you?" Cynthia reached across the table and touched the back of his hand, just for a second.

"I said we'll talk later," he snapped. "Could you please go?"

Linnet's eyes stayed on his hand after Cynthia pulled away.

"Are you two seeing each other?" she asked.

Cynthia shook her head as fast as Ethan did. "Your son is very good-looking, but I prefer a man who's more…honest."

Color fired Linnet's face. "Are you calling Ethan dishonest?"

Ethan shot his mother a warning look. They were on shaky ground, and she knew it.

"He's very good-looking," Cynthia placated her.

Linnet's fingers flexed convulsively on the table.

"Mom, I asked you here to talk about Sam." He was going to have to say it in front of Cynthia, dammit, because otherwise Linnet would lose the plot. He didn't doubt Cynthia would leave if he gave in to her request for help with the county fair, but he wasn't about to lose sight of the bigger goal, which was getting her out of the way.

"What about him? Is there another problem?" Linnet demanded.

They waited while Evie topped up their water glasses. Ethan ordered the food before he continued. He omitted Cynthia's salad, but she chipped in her request, along with a request for the meal to be served promptly because she was due back in court.

Not soon enough, as far as Ethan was concerned.

"Mom, you and I don't agree on much, but we're both worried about Sam, right?"

Linnet nodded.

"You probably see nearly as much of him as I do."

"I want him to have a safe place he can go when he's not with you," she said defensively. "I'm not trying to come between you, I wouldn't do that."

Ethan frowned. "I didn't believe you would." Cynthia was watching with interest. He rushed out what he had to say. "You and I need to pull together more with Sam when he gets up to his tricks. I want us to be allies."

"You do?" Linnet's hand fluttered to her throat. Ethan schooled himself not to make a sarcastic reply. Her excessive reactions to any overture probably weren't designed to make him look mean, they just came out that way.

"That's what I said on Sunday," Cynthia interjected.

It had been too much to hope she wouldn't

remember. "What do you think?" Ethan asked his mom.

Linnet turned to Cynthia. "This was your idea?"

She kept her gaze narrowed on Ethan. "That's right. But don't let that deter you."

"What do you think?" Ethan asked.

"I'd love to be allies," Linnet said on a sob.

"Uh, good." She wasn't about to cry, was she? No, she was happy—he recognized something of Sam in her crooked smile. "So, we have a truce?"

"Yes."

"No," Cynthia said sharply.

"I wasn't asking you." Exasperated, he shoved the basket of bread in her direction. "Put that in your mouth."

"You have a nerve," she said. "I helped you with your family problems, and you went ahead and signed me up for the judging job from hell."

"You didn't—"

"You're here because I pointed out what a great ally Linnet could be for you, and because my refusal to let Sam work at the ranch gave you an incentive to change." She looked from him to Linnet and back, her blond hair swinging.

"I would have reached the same conclusion," he said.

"I solve your problem and you try to run me out of town."

"You *are* the problem," he snapped, ignoring his mounting guilt. She was a judge, making people feel guilty was her job.

"The least you can do is help me in return." Her indignation was attracting the attention of the deputies drinking coffee at the next table.

Ethan shot to his feet. "Okay, I said we'd talk later. Turns out later is now." He jerked his head toward the door. "Mom, I'll be back in a minute. Alone."

Cynthia squeezed past Linnet to follow him out into the street. She couldn't believe she'd let Ethan make her feel so bad about Sam, when he was taking her advice all along.

"You owe me," she said when they reached the sidewalk.

He took her arm and hauled her closer to the diner window, out of the way of a group of teenagers. "Fine, I'll smile at you all you like. I'll tell people you're my friend. Satisfied?"

"Judge Merritt," a woman called.

Cynthia turned...and bit down on a groan. Tania Leach, from the *Gazette.*

"I'm glad I ran into you," Tania said. "Those extra questions..."

"I'm on my way back to court," Cynthia said. "But I can call you at four-thirty."

"Maybe just a quick chat now."

"I'm sorry." Cynthia injected regret into her smile.

"One question, then." The woman had the persistence of a migraine.

"Answer the damn question," Ethan muttered. "Get rid of her."

"Fine," Cynthia said. "Just one."

Tania smiled like the Cheshire cat. "Is it true you were forced to leave Atlanta after you had a breakdown?"

Air whistled through the space where Cynthia's stomach used to be. Her mouth worked, but no words emerged.

"A breakdown?" Ethan rocked on his feet.

"I didn't have a breakdown," Cynthia said firmly.

"So...you weren't found hiding in a broom closet?" Tania said with exaggerated delicacy.

"A closet?" Ethan echoed.

"Will you stop repeating every word she says?" Cynthia couldn't believe this reporter on a two-bit newspaper had such excellent contacts. Her father had assured her no one was talking about her failure. "I found the interim attorney general role stressful, as anyone seconded into the role with no preparation would," she told Tania. "But I didn't have a breakdown. My long-term goal has always been to make judge, and Stonewall Hollow was a great opportunity."

"Would you say your time here has also been stressful?" Tania asked.

"You've had your one question," Ethan told her. He moved closer to Cynthia.

Her knees sagged, it was all she could do not to grab his arm and cling.

The woman respected the finality in his tone in a way she hadn't with Cynthia. She departed with a promise to call later.

Cynthia leaned against the building, not caring if her suit got dirty. "Thanks," she muttered.

No reply. She looked up and found his expression harder than the brick wall at her back. "I suppose it's too much to ask for some sympathy," she said wearily.

"You're a fraud."

"I wasn't forced to leave, I chose to take a break on my father's advice."

"Because you couldn't cope." He raked a hand through his hair. "You tell me what I can and can't do with my son, you criticize me and my family, and it turns out your life is in a worse mess than mine."

"It's not." She glanced around. "Keep your voice down, people are watching."

"You don't think they deserve the truth about who's judging them?" he demanded.

"If anyone in Atlanta doubted my competence, I wouldn't be here."

"That's not true, is it?" he asked silkily. "Your family has their doubts, or you wouldn't be so worried about Tania's article."

"I meant anyone involved in my appointment," she said. "You know what families are like." She hated the note of pleading in her voice.

"Forget it." He put one hand on the wall next to her and leaned in, intimidating her. Several people in the diner looked on. "Forget any idea of me helping you. You need to get out of town fast, and the fair is a guaranteed screwup."

Cynthia's future vanished in a puff of smoke. Tania would lambaste her with impunity, and no one would defend her. The whole town would hear about the broom closet; she'd be a laughingstock, her courtroom a joke. And if that wasn't enough, the fair had disaster written all over it.

The one person with the clout to help her wanted her gone. Ten times more than he'd wanted it yesterday.

Ethan's mouth was a grim line. Who would think that he'd kissed her once? That he'd fixated on her lips as if he wanted to do it again. A lot.

She jerked away from him, only to see Mrs. Baker of pineapple upside-down cake fame over his shoulder. The woman lifted a hand in greeting, then registered the tension between Cynthia and Ethan. She turned to whisper to her friend.

"Go be a judge somewhere else," Ethan suggested. "If you want any help packing, that's one area I *am* willing to lend a hand."

A judge somewhere else. As if that would happen if she had another disgrace. She'd never work in Atlanta again....

"Of course," she said, as a blinding truth hit her.

He froze. "You want me to help you pack?"

"Uh-uh." Her mind raced. "You're going to help me on Saturday, after all."

His laugh was short and incredulous. "Dream on."

They had an audience of about twenty people now—not that Ethan could see them, facing the wall as he was. The watchers were all feigning interest in something else, yet she didn't doubt they were all soaking up the intensity of the conversation even if they couldn't hear the words. When Ethan showed the world his disdain for her at the fair, everyone would take their cue from the local hero.

"And you're damn well going to pretend you like it," she said. "Starting with this." She went up on tiptoe and pressed her mouth to his. Instinct had him kissing her back just long enough for her to wrap her arms around his neck. So when he pulled back, she moved with him.

"Cindy," he growled against her mouth. The vibration of his breath jolted her down to her toes. She clung tighter and ran her tongue along his slightly parted lips.

Just like that, everything changed. Ethan took charge, his hands anchoring her hips, his mouth coaxing hers open—not, as it turned out, a particularly challenging task. When his tongue met hers, she welcomed him with a relief that felt soul-deep.

A burst of clapping broke them apart. Ethan spun around, then back to Cynthia, dazed but glowering. "It won't take a second for me to set everyone straight."

She grabbed a fistful of his shirt. "You do that and you'll never be rid of me."

His eyebrows drew together in a dark slash.

"I'm under consideration for a judgeship in the superior court in Atlanta," she said rapidly. "If I mess up here, I won't get the job."

"I don't give a damn—"

"It's your best chance of me leaving," she told him. "There aren't dozens of people lining up to be Stonewall Hollow's judge. You heard Sally, Judge Piet's health is getting worse. I can probably stay on as long as I like."

His eyes seared her as he processed the implications. He clenched his teeth.

Cynthia let go of his shirt and sidestepped around him. "Nine o'clock Saturday in the cake tent," she said. "See you then."

With a jaunty wave to the audience, she headed back to court.

Chapter Ten

Cynthia's cell phone rang on her way up the courthouse's marble staircase.

She checked the display, then pressed to answer. "Megan, hi."

"Hey, Cynthia." Her sister's voice produced a pang of homesickness, and a sudden, shaking reaction to her conversation with Ethan. Cynthia tightened her grip on the phone.

"Sabrina's with me, we have you on speaker," Megan said.

"Hi, Cyn," Sabrina called.

"Is something wrong—is Dad okay?" Cynthia crossed the landing, passed Melanie's desk and entered her chambers. She closed the door behind her.

Sabrina laughed, the sound that drew people to her like sailors to a Siren. "We just wanted to talk. I came into Megan's office for lunch so we could chat just as if you were here."

Which they'd never have done if Cynthia was in the city. As lawyers at Merritt, Merritt & Finch, she and Megan had always been far too busy for midweek chitchat. Cynthia slung her purse over the back of her chair. She sank into the maroon leather.

"Give us the scoop on small-town life," Megan demanded.

In a moment of panic, Cynthia swiveled to the window. Of course her sister wasn't outside, didn't know anything about what had just happened. But Megan had excellent instincts, in court and out.

"Everything's going fine." She wished she wasn't so pathetically committed to being the best that she couldn't be honest with Megan, who she was closer to than anyone. Other than Dad.

"I knew you'd make a great judge," Sabrina said with her usual immense capacity for loyalty and for giving people the benefit of the doubt. "I'd love to see you in action on the bench."

"You always say black washes me out."

Sabrina, the undisputed fashion expert, laughed.

Cynthia needed to steer the conversation away from all potentially dangerous topics. Such as her career, her adjustment to Stonewall Hollow, her desire to return home. Pretty much her whole life. "How are you two, anyway?"

"Great." Sabrina's answer was more dreamy sigh than conversation. She and Jake had been married six months.

"Greater," Megan said, an uncharacteristic giggle escaping her. Megan had married her husband, Travis, just a month ago. They'd only been back from their honeymoon a week before Cynthia left Atlanta.

It was an old game of theirs—Great, Greater, Greatest. Cynthia would have killed—if it hadn't been illegal—to have a man in her life who would allow her to chip in with "Greatest."

Desperate kisses forced onto men who didn't like her didn't qualify.

Cynthia skimmed the afternoon's case docket as she listened to her sisters' news, which mainly involved their plans for blissful futures with their true loves.

"Met any nice guys down there?" Sabrina asked, with the newlywed's enthusiasm for inducting others to the married state.

She recalled the sensuous feel of Ethan's mouth. "Uh…"

"I can't see Cynthia with some hick," Megan said.

She remembered Ethan's hand against the wall next to her shoulder. In her peripheral vision she'd noted a strong, tanned forearm with exactly the right amount of hair. His white T-shirt had molded to muscle gained through hard work. His masculine face was rugged, with intriguing planes.

"So what do you do in your spare time?" Megan asked, making her feel more than ever like the spinster sister.

I knit socks for the troops. "Actually, I'm involved in the county fair," she said. "I'm judging the contests. Cakes, pets, babies, you name it."

"Wow," Sabrina said. "I'd have said you didn't know the difference between those things."

Cynthia surprised herself by laughing.

"You want to be careful," Sabrina cautioned. "Remember my pumpkin killer."

"I'll be fine," Cynthia said. "I'll have help." She hoped.

"Maybe we should come visit," Megan suggested. "We'll provide moral support, and celebrate the Fourth at the same time."

"No," Cynthia said sharply. Ethan's cooperation was far from guaranteed, and if things were going to go wrong, she didn't need witnesses. She went to get her robe from the hook on the door.

"Cynthia, sweetie, are you okay?" Sabrina asked.

She didn't need her *baby* sister treating her with kid gloves.

"I'd love to see you guys, but I'll be so busy with the judging on Saturday—" she swapped the phone from one hand to the other as she wriggled into the robe "—I won't have time to even notice your support, let alone enjoy it."

"I guess that's true," Megan said.

Phew.

"So...you're definitely okay?" Megan continued.

"Perfect," Cynthia lied. Because the truth—*I'm jealous of my sisters, I'm fending off cake bribes, and if Ethan won't help me I'll be public enemy number one by Monday*—wasn't acceptable to her family. Or her.

Cynthia wore her yellow sundress to the fair on Saturday, not the judicial robes Jackson had suggested. A message not to take this too seriously. She hoped people would get it, loud and clear. So that if she screwed up… *I can't screw up.*

En route to the cake tent she hurried past the carnival rides and fast-food stands without pausing. When she saw the stressed-out mothers lining up outside the big top for the baby and toddler pageant, she shuddered. What had she been thinking?

"All ready, Judge?" Jackson Bream was resplendent in a white suit, pale pink shirt and black string tie.

"Absolutely," she fibbed. "Uh, is Ethan here?"

Jackson's sly look said he'd heard about their public kiss. "Not yet."

"I'll wait for him." An entirely unwarranted leap of faith.

They made small talk for a minute, but it wasn't her forte and soon dried up. Jackson handed her a clipboard thick with pages.

"These are your entry lists—quite straightforward. You give each entry a score. Top three place. We'll start the moment you're ready."

"When Ethan gets here." Cynthia scanned the lists with rising dread. She'd bitten off more than she could chew: more cake, more pie, more cookies, more preserves. "I don't see the babies."

"Ethan told me you couldn't do the babies," he said.

She stared. "Wh-when?"

"Yesterday afternoon. I asked my sister to stand in," Jackson informed her. "She's done it before and she hates it, but she's a retired pediatrician so she knows her stuff."

"So Ethan's really coming," she said, dazed.

He eyed her curiously. "If you want the babies back..."

"No," she said quickly.

"Once you've made your choices," Jackson said, "my staff will complete the certificates and find the appropriate trophy or ribbon. Which you'll hand over."

"Right before you skip town," Ethan said behind her.

Cynthia tried to compose herself before she

turned around, but she was so pleased to see him, her grin must have been a mile wide. "Not going to happen," she reminded him. "Not yet."

How could a simple pair of jeans look as if they'd been made for him? A plaid shirt fit like Armani? His hat sat low on his forehead, giving him a dangerous air.

Or maybe the danger was in his eyes. She couldn't read his expression…but when his eyes dipped to her lips, she let out a breath of relief. If he was still distracted by that kiss, he couldn't be too angry.

"I suggest you start right here with the cakes," Jackson said. "The ladies don't like it if their frosting sits in the sun too long. Finish with the preserves—they've been hanging around two years already, another few hours won't hurt."

The cake table held at least thirty entries: chocolate cakes, banana, lemon, sponge and—surprise, surprise—a pineapple upside-down cake.

Jackson handed her a cake knife. "A small taste of each."

"And after that, I need to taste the cookies and the pies and the preserves?"

"That's right."

Cynthia fanned the pages on her clipboard. They went on forever.

"You don't have to taste the bonsai," Ethan said helpfully.

Jackson chuckled. "Now, if you'll excuse me, I'm needed over at the main stage."

Cynthia handed Ethan the knife. "You can do the cutting." She swallowed. "Partner."

He looked down at the knife for a long moment, as if contemplating all its potential uses. Then he jabbed it into a triple-layer chocolate confection that had the number 001 printed on the card next to it.

She closed her eyes in momentary relief. When she opened them, Ethan was holding out a morsel of cake on the knife.

She took it, turned it over to examine it from all sides. "It looks perfect."

"Things aren't always what they seem. Sometimes they don't live up to the high standard they present to the world."

Cynthia hoped he wasn't setting the tone for the whole day. She popped the cake in her mouth, eyes closed. Let the frosting melt on her tongue. Chewed. Swallowed. "It *is* perfect. Sometimes, appearances are right."

With effort, she dragged her eyes from Ethan down to her score sheet. Cake 001, top of the page. The maximum score was thirty. After a moment's hesitation, she filled in her score.

He read over her shoulder. "You're giving it full marks?"

She turned her head…and found his mouth inches from hers. "Um…"

"Was it really that great?" His gaze hung on her lips.

"Maybe it wasn't," she said. "I don't eat a lot of cake. Maybe it was only average. Mediocre, even."

He frowned. "Or maybe it was incredible."

"I think I'll give it twenty-eight. In case it wasn't the best." She amended the score, then ran the back of her hand across her forehead. This tent was already sweltering.

The next cake was an orange cake, beautifully scented, the frosting flecked with orange zest. "Full marks," Cynthia murmured. She licked a crumb off her lips.

Ethan watched the progress of her tongue. "Is it better than the first one?"

"I guess it's about the same." She scored the orange cake twenty-eight, too. "I guess there's not much difference between one cake and another."

He cut another piece of the cake and sampled it himself. Then did the same with the chocolate cake. "The orange one," he said. "It's in a league of its own."

She focused on her score sheet. "The problem with cake is it's not good for you."

"No," he agreed.

The air crackled. On edge, Cynthia shifted, and one of her sundress straps slid off her shoulder. Ethan's gaze settled on the bared flesh. "Knowing something's not good for you doesn't necessarily stop you wanting it."

Cynthia clutched her clipboard to her chest. "We need to move on."

Every single cake tasted perfect, as good as it looked. Soon, Cynthia had a page full of twenty-fives to twenty-eights, with a lone carrot cake scoring twenty-four because the cream cheese frosting was too runny.

With the tent open on all sides in a vain attempt to dissipate the heat, judging was a very visible process. When people realized Cynthia had started, she attracted a crowd of hangers-on. Ethan spent much time politely but firmly fending off women who were determined to read over her shoulder. That meant he stayed close to her, which made it difficult to concentrate.

More than once she heard, "They make

such a cute couple." If Ethan heard, he didn't show it.

After the last cake, Cynthia showed Ethan the score sheet.

"You have twelve cakes in first place," he said, incredulous. "Seven in second, nine in—"

"I know, I know." She slapped the clipboard in frustration, causing a ripple of concern among the bystanders. "But they were all wonderful." Or maybe it was just that every one of her senses had been bizarrely heightened all morning. "How do people feel about multiple winners?"

"You'll be lynched," he said.

"That's what I thought."

He met her worried glance, and took a step back. "We need a more technical approach. You judge things all the time."

"There are laws in court," she said. "That's what I judge people against."

"Then find some laws that work here."

"Cakes as defendants," Cynthia said slowly. She paced the length of the cake table, clipboard banging absently against her thigh. "We can cross-examine them."

"Isn't cross-examining a cake one step short of hiding in a broom closet?" he asked.

She froze, then spurted a laugh. "I can't answer that on the grounds it might incriminate me."

Just when she thought it wasn't possible for a man to get any sexier, his smile crinkled the edges of his eyes.

Ethan informed Jackson that they needed a short recess from judging. They headed to the office behind the rodeo arena, one of the few permanent buildings on the site, where they sat down with pen and paper.

"I'll use a grid," Cynthia said. "Maximum fifty points, so there's not as much likelihood of multiple entries getting the same score."

"What's on the grid?"

She frowned. "Cakey qualities, I guess. Taste, smell, appearance..."

"Texture," Ethan suggested. "A good cake is moist."

Moist, she wrote. Then crossed it out and replaced it with *Texture*.

Within half an hour they had grids for every contest. It was time to return to the fray.

It was a breeze. Apart from having to retaste all the cakes, which at least scored Cynthia kudos for her thoroughness. It was much easier to award marks out of ten on each criterion, rather than pick a random number out of fifty.

Cynthia didn't add each cake's score as she went, so she didn't know who'd won until Ethan totaled the numbers. The orange cake won first place, with a Black Forest gateau and a ginger cake tied for second. A banana cake came fourth.

Jackson posted the entire grid on the bulletin board, and the women pored over it long enough for Cynthia to get through the pies and the cookies.

By the time she got to preserves, she was on a roll. "Let me know when I have to skip town," she told Ethan as she sliced into her twelfth pickled onion. She inspected it. "This one's an eight on appearance. It's amazing how different each pickled onion is. They're practically human."

He threw back his head and laughed. "Spoken like a girl from onion country."

"Three days ago you told me I don't fit in here."

He paused. Then he tucked his hand under her elbow. "Your next pickle awaits, Your Honor."

The only reason he's helping is because

he wants me to get the superior court job, so I'll leave town.

She pulled out of his grasp and forged ahead.

By the time the day ended, Cynthia was stuffed, exhausted and she had heartburn from the pickles and preserves. But the crowd cheered her after she presented the cups and no one issued a death threat. Best of all, Tania from the *Gazette* interviewed her, along with several happy contestants. The reporter grudgingly told her she'd done a good job.

It was six o'clock by the time she and Ethan strolled out of the fairground into the parking lot.

"Judge Merritt!" The shrill call came from Mrs. Baker, whose pineapple upside-down cake had placed seventh. Puffing, she caught up to them next to Cynthia's car. "We're having a cake and coffee session later with the leftovers. We'd love for you to join us."

Eat more food? But this was the friendliest overture she'd had since she arrived in Stonewall Hollow. Cynthia couldn't think of a way to refuse without giving offence.

"The judge is having dinner with me tonight," Ethan said.

Just like that, Mrs. Baker beamed. "Of

course she is, how lovely. You two have a wonderful evening—don't give our little soiree a single thought."

Cynthia protested politely, and the older woman left in good spirits.

"Thanks," Cynthia said to Ethan. "If I sneak home and leave my lights off all evening, no one will know I wasn't out with you."

"Let's have dinner," he said, and looked as surprised as she felt.

Her pulse sped up. "I've been eating all day."

"I witnessed every bite," he reminded her. "You need something savory."

"Pickles are savory." Why was she arguing, when she wanted to go with him?

"If you get that job this could be our last chance for a meal together."

That was why she was arguing. Because he still wanted her gone.

He touched a finger to the underside of her chin. "Cindy."

He'd been calling her that all day. "It's Cynthia."

He kissed her, a lingering, experimental kiss. A delicious tension built inside her.

"Let's go to dinner," he said.

Chapter Eleven

Ethan followed Cindy—he couldn't help it, he just didn't think of her as a Cynthia—back to her place, where they left her car. They went to dinner in his truck.

"We'll drive to Gonville," Ethan said. "You could do without the world watching your every move tonight." He didn't want the world intruding, either. All damn day he'd been so turned on by her—hell, ever since she'd planted that kiss on him outside Sally's. He wanted to kiss her again. Make love to her. She wanted the same. He heard it in the hitch of her breath when he got close to her, saw it in the flare of interest in her eyes, in the sensual curve of her mouth when she'd smiled at him today.

They had their differences, but with her about to leave town, he'd bet they could both overlook them.

Gonville was in Myers County, a half-hour drive along the highway that skirted the plain. The town was newer than Stonewall Hollow, with five times the population.

The restaurant he chose, the Red Shed, was more sophisticated than its name suggested. On the outside, it did resemble a barn, but the riverbank setting was charming. Inside, it was all high ceilings, fancy light fixtures and white tablecloths.

The waiter brought them menus, handwritten in silver ink. Cindy sat back and inhaled the pervasive aroma of garlic and basil. "Just the fact that I don't have to score the food means I'm having a great time already."

"You're a cheap date."

When she pointedly ordered the lobster, Ethan laughed and did the same. He chose a buttery, vanilla-scented chardonnay to match the food.

He lifted his glass. "To new horizons."

She set her glass down with a thud. "Will

you stop counting the minutes until I leave town?"

Whoa, where had that come from? "I wasn't." It might be premature to admit he'd meant a new level of intimacy between them, among other things. "You're the one who wants an important new job."

She hesitated, but she clinked her glass against his.

"Was today enough to get you the job?" he asked. "Which I'm not asking because I'm counting the minutes."

She shrugged. "Too soon to say. But it will certainly keep my father happy."

"You really believe he cares about what the Stonewall Hollow newspaper says about you?"

"Dad retired after a heart attack last year, and we've been spending quite a bit of time together—he's a genius at career planning. He'd love for me to get a position with the superior court. He'd be disappointed if some reporter put an end to the dream."

He heard the deep love in her voice. "He must have hated having you move so far away."

"I—" She fiddled with her knife and fork. "It was Dad's idea for me to come here." She added lightly, "A lesson not to hide in broom closets."

"You mean, what Tania said is true? You were forced to leave Atlanta."

The waiter brought their lobsters, along with extra napkins and finger bowls.

"Dad *recommended* I leave." Cindy rearranged her finger bowl and unfolded a couple of napkins. "I used to—when I was a kid, when Mom and Dad fought—I used to hide in the closet. Something about the dark and the quiet made all my troubles go away." She straightened. "But when you do it as an adult, it's more of a big deal."

"Will it be a big deal to your dad if you don't get the job?" he asked.

"It's a big deal to *me,*" she said sharply. Then she admitted, "I'm not sure what we'd talk about if I wasn't in some high-flying position."

Ethan forked some lobster. "How about the same as he talks to your sisters about?"

"It's *not* the same," she said. "Dad and I have always had a special bond. I don't want to lose it."

"What kind of relationship is that? Where you're scared to step out of line, or to be less than perfect?"

"It's the only one I've got." She clapped a hand over her mouth.

Ethan shifted in his seat. *Find something else to talk about.* "Are your sisters like you?"

She nodded her approval of the new topic, as if they were in court. "I'm the bossy one. Megan's a lawyer, supersharp but very sweet when you get to know her. Sabrina—she's technically my half sister—is gorgeous. Though Megan's pretty, too," she added.

"And you're a turnip-face, I suppose."

She snorted her chardonnay and had to blow her nose. "I am not a turnip-face."

"My point exactly," he said.

"But Sabrina was Miss Georgia."

"*That* Sabrina? Wait a minute, isn't she married to the governor?"

"My brother-in-law Jake."

"You said both your sisters got married recently," he remembered. "You didn't sound that happy about it."

She colored. "Of course I'm happy. They both found wonderful men."

"But…?" he prompted.

"I got drunk at both their weddings," she confessed, and then sipped her wine defiantly.

Ethan laughed. "I'll bet you're cute when you're drunk."

"I'm maudlin," she corrected him. "And jealous. It's pitiful."

He poured some melted butter over his lobster. "You want to get married?"

Her shocked silence made him look up.

"That wasn't a proposal, right?" she asked.

Ethan knocked the jug of butter, and only just managed to save it from spilling across the table. "I don't even know you. And I don't want to get married. To anyone."

"Okay, I get the message." Her cheeks were a deeper red now. "It was just the weird way you said it."

He replayed his own words. He didn't see any room for confusion.

"To answer your question," she said. "I do want to get married. But not just to anyone."

"You have high standards, of course." Ethan dug more lobster out of the shell. "A millionaire lawyer, at the very least."

"No, thanks," she said. "I'll settle for a man who loves me for who I am and isn't afraid to show it."

"That sounds so simple, there has to be a catch."

She laughed. It was a carefree sound, and it lightened Ethan's heart. Too bad they wouldn't have long for this fling of theirs.

"No catch," she said. "Just a simple, honest man."

Ah. There was the catch.

"Why don't you want to get married?" She ground black pepper over her meal.

He shrugged. "My life is a mess, as you haven't hesitated to tell me." It was certainly not *simple.* "It's hard enough keeping a relationship going with Mom and Sam. Maybe one day, after I get the hang of that..."

"Don't you want to have more kids?" she asked.

"I'd sure like to have one from birth. Maybe even two or three. Give me a chance to get it right before I get it wrong."

"Your mom must have been very young when she had you," Cindy observed.

"She was seventeen," he said. "The guy who knocked her up had left town to go to college by the time I arrived."

"So...your father wasn't a regular fixture in your life?"

"He never came back to Augusta. His parents moved away later, too, but they sent money. They were just ordinary folks, so it wasn't a lot, but we weren't destitute."

"Did you ever try to find your father?" She

sat back while the waiter refilled her wineglass.

"I kept up with his whereabouts," Ethan said. "He worked as an accountant, married, had three kids. Mom wrote him once a year, telling him where we were, what we were doing. We're not in contact now."

Cynthia was amazed at the parallels between his life and Sam's. But she was pretty sure Linnet hadn't been a supportive parent like he was to Sam. "Did your mom ever marry?"

She read his desire to clam up. Then he spread his fingers loosely on the table and said, "When I was four, she married my stepfather. Wayne. He was mean, controlling and a bully."

"Did he hit her?" she asked, horrified.

Ethan shook his head. "He could control her without violence. He hit me, always under the guise of discipline, but I saw his pleasure. He loved it."

He dug back into his lobster. Cynthia waited, afraid he wouldn't say more.

"Mom always took Wayne's side," Ethan finally said. "If she'd just once told him to leave me alone, I could have handled it. Maybe. But she wouldn't confront him. As you noticed, she has trouble confronting anyone head-on. Instead, I turned about as mean as he was. I was at best obnoxious and antisocial.

"At worst, I had a gang of so-called friends held together by trouble and the sense of power that came with causing it. It was the only control we had over our lives."

"Were you…in trouble with the law?"

"Over and over." Ethan's rueful expression told her he knew she was comparing him and Sam. "It drove Mom crazy, much worse than anything Wayne did. She threw me out when I turned eighteen, which meant I had to leave school."

"You didn't graduate?" She would never have picked him as uneducated.

He wiped his mouth with his napkin. "I did later. Back then, I just had to survive. I went to Atlanta, took whatever work I could get, slept rough when I had to, bunked with friends."

"I can't imagine any mother washing her hands of her son," Cynthia said fiercely.

"We've both struggled to get past it," he admitted. "Even though Mom divorced Wayne after—soon after I left town, I never forgave her for marrying the guy in the first place."

"You said love isn't about what someone

does or doesn't do. It's about who they are in your life. She's your mother. You're her son. In theory, that should be enough."

He frowned. "I never said I was right about that."

"I think you are. What's stopping you and Linnet from getting over the past?"

"Partly it's that we both hate talking about it," he admitted.

"You're talking to me."

"That's because you're the nosiest woman I ever met."

She reached across and touched his wrist. "Thank you."

He turned his hand over and entwined her fingers in his. "And because I want to go to bed with you."

Cynthia caught her breath. "That's...honest."

"I don't know why I'm telling you as much as I have," he added.

"The, uh, bed thing," she prompted.

"That, of course." He smiled that crinkly smile again, then sobered. "I hate the way I was back then, on an emotional roller coaster. I was so mad, I did a bunch of things I regret. I don't want to feel that angry again."

"You wouldn't react the same now," she

said. "I've seen a lot of nasty guys in my time as a defense lawyer. I know what unrepentant, untamed anger looks like, and believe me, you have nothing in common with these guys."

He withdrew his hand, folded his arms. "It's not a risk I want to take."

His shutdown was so sudden, Cynthia was left floundering for words. Hadn't he just been telling her he wanted to make love to her? You wouldn't think it to see the flatness in his eyes. Finally, she asked, "How did you end up in Stonewall Hollow?"

He hesitated. "I met a guy, Paul Siddons. He and his wife, Debbie, owned the Double T. Paul offered me a job. I was desperate, so I took it, though I couldn't imagine anything I'd like less." He smiled at the memory. "I loved it, from the get-go. When Paul retired, he and Debbie went to live in Canada near their daughter. They sold me the ranch, gave me a mortgage when the bank wouldn't. I'm still paying them off, but in a couple of years I'll own the place free and clear."

"That's quite a road you've traveled," she said. "From being thrown out of home, to owning a ranch."

"The Siddonses taught me a lot about decency, about trust, about hanging in for the long haul. I've tried to live that, and to pass it on to other people."

"I admire how far you've come," she said slowly, "but you can't tell me you weren't hurt, terribly, when Linnet threw you out. That's how Sam must feel about his mom now. He must be in agony."

Ethan jerked back in his seat. "It's not the same. Susan sent Sam to me. To his father. She didn't leave him to fend for himself."

"He doesn't necessarily feel as if you're his father."

"I'm working on that." He drew in a breath. "Cindy—"

"Cynthia," she corrected automatically. She wasn't sure how she felt about him calling her Cindy. It sounded more relaxed than she ever was…which had a certain appeal.

"Cindy," he repeated, "don't spoil this evening by bringing up our disagreements over Sam."

"What, you think I'll ruin your plan to get me into bed?"

The waiter had just arrived at their table; he turned on his heel and left.

"You scared him off," Ethan said. "Won't be so easy to get rid of me."

* * *

"Coffee?" Cynthia offered as she set her purse down on the kitchen counter in her cottage.

Ethan prowled the room, looking as hungry as if they hadn't just had an enormous meal. "No."

He'd held her hand on his thigh the whole way home from Gonville; she could still feel the heat of his leg against her palm. She led the way to the living room, where he joined her on the old corduroy couch.

He kissed her.

Oh, yes. His hands cupped her head, his mouth was warm and coaxing and inviting. When his tongue flicked against her lips, she parted them immediately. Ethan eased her back against the cushions.

She'd never felt such intense desire for a man. Was this the way Sabrina felt about Jake? Megan about Travis? This consuming combination of physical longing and a deep, honest connection?

Ethan's hands moved down to her butt, and she arched to meet him. Still, she needed to be closer. She wrapped her arms around his neck, pressed against him, and he groaned.

Ethan ran kisses along her jawline, then

dropped his lips to her neck, her collarbone. His hands came up to her waist…where his watch snagged on the fabric of her dress. He muttered a curse. “This isn’t the kind of dress I can tear off you, right?”

“No,” she agreed reluctantly. “It’s the only nonwork dress I have here.”

As he disentangled the offending watch, then slipped it off, she tried to think sensibly about whether her dress should come off tonight at all.

“I’m now free to wander.” He showed her his bare wrist, then his finger traced her eyebrows, her nose, down over her mouth to her chin. “You’re so beautiful.”

As his mouth explored hers again and his hands swept her curves, she tugged his shirt up, fanned her fingers on the taut skin of his back.

She lost track of time in the haze his caresses induced, in the seeking heat of his mouth. When they broke apart, her limbs were like jelly. She had no volition beyond responding to Ethan.

While she’d been lost in that kiss, her fingers had been greedily pushing his shirt buttons through their holes. His bare chest was a beautiful sight. She reached out and touched. "The bed thing," she started.

He shuddered beneath her fingers. "What about it?"

"You're not looking for a serious relationship."

"Neither are you," he said. "You're leaving town."

She kissed his shoulder. "All I want is to know how you feel."

He laced her fingers through his, brought her knuckles to his mouth and nipped. Sensation shot through her. "What do you mean?"

"I don't think expressing your feelings comes naturally to you," she said. "At least it doesn't with Sam."

He tensed. "We're not talking about Sam. And he understands how I feel."

Now wasn't the time to argue that. "But I don't like second-guessing you," she said. "I'm not asking for undying devotion or anything. I just need to know where I stand at any given time."

"And, uh, how would you expect to figure that out?"

She smiled against his neck. "You would tell me. Honestly and simply."

"That sounds reasonable." He took her mouth again, dragging her into a deep kiss.

"So," she managed to say some time later, "how do you feel about me?"

He lifted his head from the inside of her knee, a spot she'd never realized was so sensitive. "You want me to tell you now?"

She blinked. "That's what I've been explaining to you."

"You mean, *right* now?"

She scrambled up on the cushions. "Ethan, I told you. It doesn't matter how you feel, as long as you don't leave me in the dark. You can be honest."

He shot upright. "No way."

"No way you won't be honest?" She tugged her skirt down from around her thighs.

"I'm not doing this," he said. "I'm not getting into a situation where I can screw up yet another relationship."

"If you're honest, what can possibly go wrong?" Problems, she realized, occurred when you didn't know what someone else expected of you. When you loved them but weren't sure they loved you back.

"There are a million things that can go wrong." He began buttoning his shirt. "This isn't how you start a relationship, even a casual one. You don't decide how you feel on day one. It takes time to figure that stuff out."

"And even longer to say it," she suggested.

"Maybe," he said warily.

"The eleven years it's taken you to not tell your mother how you feel?" she demanded. "Or the eighteen years for Sam?"

"I didn't know Sam," he snapped.

"All the more reason to do some catching up."

"Why are we talking about this?" he said. "From day one you've been in my family's face. Just drop it, Cynthia. I don't need you butting in."

"Fine," she snapped. "Let's just drop everything."

"Fine," he said, as he walked out the door.

"Fine," she muttered as his car pulled out of her driveway.

Chapter Twelve

It was one thing kissing a man, half undressing him late at night after a few glasses of wine. It was another to face him in daylight, after he'd refused to make love to you.

As Cynthia spread her toast with Melanie's homemade strawberry jam on Sunday morning, she considered staying away from the Fourth of July rodeo. The thought of the you-nearly-saw-me-naked awkwardness with Ethan was unbearable.

She missed him already, the stubborn, uncommunicative jerk. He'd said he didn't want complications so she'd made it as simple as possible. Didn't matter what he felt, all he had to do was tell her. So she wouldn't end up feeling the way she did with her family. Insecure. But he couldn't even do that.

She was halfway through brushing her teeth when the doorbell rang.

Ethan! Her heart leaped. Maybe he'd spent a sleepless night, like her, and decided he could tell her what he felt. That he couldn't afford not to.

Her toothbrush clattered into the sink. She defoamed, shimmied out of her ratty pajamas and pulled on white denim shorts and a pink tank top.

The doorbell rang again. "Coming," she called, as she tugged a brush through her hair. She slowed as she reached the bottom of the stairs, took a calming breath, pinned on a smile.

She opened the door.

"Surprise!" her sisters chorused.

Travis and Jake, her brothers-in-law, stood behind Megan and Sabrina, grinning, crowding her porch.

Cynthia felt a sting of disappointment as she hugged both girls, followed by guilt, panic and, belatedly, pleasure in seeing her family.

"What are you doing here? It's so great

to see you." She stepped aside so they could troop into the cottage.

"Wow, look at this place," Sabrina said. "So cute."

"Take off your rose-colored spectacles, darling," Jake said. "It's a dump."

Sabrina swatted him. "It has character."

"Sorry about the mess, I overslept." Cynthia waved apologetically at the breakfast clutter. "If I'd known you were coming..."

"You said you were busy with your fair judging yesterday, but we figured we could spend the Fourth—" Megan stopped. She'd been scanning the room more objectively than Sabrina, and obviously she'd found something. Megan had always been part-bloodhound. Was there an Ethan-shaped dent in the cushions? Cynthia didn't want to look.

Travis, who knew Megan better than she knew herself, squeezed his wife's hand and gave Cynthia a sympathetic look. Her stomach lurched. "How about us guys make coffee," he suggested. "Come on, Jake."

"Hey, I'm the governor. People bring *me* coffee," Jake protested.

"I'm helping you keep you in touch with the little people," Travis said.

Grumbling good-naturedly, Jake followed

him into the kitchen. The door closed behind the two men.

"So," Megan said, "which man left his watch on your couch in a moment of passion?"

Sabrina squawked. "Where?" She dived for the couch, fishing out Ethan's watch. "Ohh, let's take a look." She examined the face. "Timex."

Cynthia blushed, as if it would be more acceptable to have a Rolex or a TAG Heuer stuffed into her sofa. Then she blushed deeper because she remembered the delicious touch of Ethan's watchless hand. She blushed beyond belief when she remembered how he'd walked out, not caring enough to find words to say to her.

"Who is he?" Megan demanded. "You're beet-red."

"I'm not," Cynthia said. "And he's…no one."

"How long is it since you had a date, let alone loosened up enough to make out on the couch?" Sabrina pushed a strand of blond hair behind her ear, her blue eyes wide beneath perfectly shaped brows. "This guy is someone, Cynthia."

That's what she was starting to worry about. "There's not a lot else to do in this place," she prevaricated. "Look, he's a nice guy, we went out for dinner, we kissed."

"And it was hot," Sabrina said helpfully.

"Yes, it was hot." Just like her cheeks. "But it was only a kiss."

"So...you're not dating him?" Sabrina sounded disappointed. "Why not?"

Because he thinks I'm too complicated. "It's difficult. He's involved in the justice system, and I'm the only judge."

"He's not in trouble with the law?" Megan's forehead creased with her determination not to overreact. But she nibbled on her lower lip.

"Someone close to him is. It's a major conflict."

"Conflict of interest is no excuse for giving up," Sabrina said. "Look at Megan and Travis."

Megan cleared her throat—she was never entirely comfortable with the reminder she'd met her husband when they were working opposite sides of a divorce case.

Cynthia seized the opportunity to change the subject. "How's Dad?" She snatched Ethan's watch from Sabrina and wedged it into the pocket of her shorts.

"He sends his love," Megan said. "As soon as he heard we were going out of town, he set up a golf weekend. But he wants to hear *everything* you're up to."

Cynthia shivered. Only about five percent of what had happened since she arrived in Stonewall Hollow was fit for Jonah's ears. She plumped up the cushions on the couch. "So what would you guys like to do while you're here? I can show you around the courthouse." She didn't want to encounter Ethan in front of her family, and that's one place he wouldn't be today.

Sabrina stuck out a foot and lifted the long skirt of her sundress. "We're here for the rodeo. I bought these boots especially." Lime-green cowboy boots with three-inch heels.

Cynthia had to laugh. "Okay, I guess it's the rodeo, then." She had a moment of panic… what if she'd overestimated her success yesterday, and people still didn't like her? What if they liked her sisters better? What if *Ethan* liked her sisters better? *Ethan doesn't matter.* "If you get bored, we can come back here."

Megan grinned. "I won't be bored, I'll be on the lookout for a guy who's lost his watch."

Jake came back into the room with mugs, cream and sugar. Travis followed, carrying a pot of coffee. "Still harassing your sister, Megs?" Travis dropped a kiss on Megan's lips.

"Almost done," she said. He shook his head with a silent warning. They'd only been married just over a month, but Cynthia was always amazed how well Travis seemed to know his wife.

He served the coffee and they settled on every available seat, with Sabrina perched on the coffee table.

"We have news," Megan said. "Good news."

Cynthia gasped. "You're having a baby?" Megan had always sworn she didn't want kids, but she'd noticeably softened on that stance since she met Travis. She and Travis job-shared the managing partner role at Merritt, Merritt & Finch, an arrangement Cynthia assumed was intended to one day accommodate a kid-friendly lifestyle.

"Good news for *you,*" Megan amended. "Dad got a call late last night." She paused for effect.

"Spit it out," Cynthia said.

"Judge Fisher has brought forward his retirement," Megan announced. "His wife wants a round-the-world trip for their golden wedding, so he's finishing mid-August. There'll be an announcement soon."

"I guess they'll be speeding up the appointment of a new judge." Cynthia sipped on her coffee, while she dug into the couch cushion with the fingers of her left hand. So soon? She could be out of here? Maybe without ever having to face Ethan...that was patently ridiculous, she quashed the thought.

"You guessed it. And the great news is, Justice Pearson has taken over as head of the nominating committee."

Hal Pearson was one of their father's oldest friends. Not a golf and fishing buddy, but a friendship born of a long time spent as colleagues, bolstered by shared views on most issues.

"Dad's been talking to Hal about you, and Hal is—" Megan made quote marks "'—intrigued.' And impressed by what Dad calls your determination to understand the needs of smaller communities." Her smile was sympathetically mocking.

"I was *banished*."

"Dad's view is Hal didn't need to know every detail," Megan said. "Best not to use the *B* word when he visits."

Cynthia slopped her coffee. "When he *what?*"

Sabrina went to get a cloth, ignoring Jake's attempts to have her stay where she was.

"If Hal recommends you to the committee, he needs to do so in good faith, not just because he's a friend of Dad's. He plans to come down Thursday the fifteenth for an informal chat. Then he'll sit in on a court session."

Cynthia had ten days to perfect her performance. Ten days to keep everyone in town on her side. Ten days to avoid Ethan….

"Cyn?" Megan eyed her curiously over the rim of her mug—she'd said something Cynthia had missed. "Dad wants to know if you're in session that day—that it's not Stonewall Hollow Independence Day or something."

"I'm in session," Cynthia said woodenly.

Megan's eyes softened. "Hal won't expect you to start off in the superior court a hundred percent perfect. You'll be mentored by a more experienced judge."

"This is what you want, isn't it?" Sabrina chipped in as she wiped the spilled coffee. "You don't think it'll be too stressful?"

"Of course it's what I want," Cynthia said. Her answer would go directly back to Jonah. Inside, she felt like the rope in the tug-of-war at the fair yesterday.

The pull of home, of her dad and the plans they'd made versus the pull of her realization that those things weren't enough.

* * *

Ethan had been watching for Cindy since the minute he got to the rodeo. He'd wanted to stop by her place on his way in, but with Sam in the truck, sullen in the extreme, it didn't seem wise.

Last night's dinner, then those kisses, those caresses. Mind-blowing. Too mind-blowing. Every instinct screamed he was out of his depth, no matter what tripe he'd told Cindy about not wanting complications.

It scared the hell out of him. Look what a damn-awful job he was doing with his mom and Sam, barely keeping his temper half the time. But he'd realized last night he might not be able to let Cindy go. He wanted her in a way that transcended any other desire he knew.

Talk about triple complications. He couldn't begin to explore those thoughts without telling Cindy the truth. Confessing, to use the legal jargon.

He wasn't about to confess here at the rodeo, but he could ask her for another date. Another chance. Hell, how many chances did a guy have to get it right?

Ethan glanced at his wrist and for the tenth time that morning found it bare. In the arena, they'd finished the senior grade competition, so it had to be nearly eleven.

He turned back to watch the presentation of prizes to the seniors. A cheer went up after each award. The weather couldn't be better and the crowd was ready to applaud just about anything.

Ethan drummed his fingers on the rail. The arena was noisy, with announcements and commentary feeding through the PA system, the crowd and all the animals. Behind him, the jingle music of carnival rides and the shrieks of overexcited kids filled the air.

He looked around for Sam. Over at the other side of the arena, Linnet was talking to Sally from the diner. Sensing his gaze, she turned. Her unguarded smile took Ethan by surprise; he found himself smiling back, tipping his hat. Huh.

"Dad."

His heart jolted in his chest at Sam's voice. Sam didn't often call him Dad. Usually it was just *Hey.* "What's up?" Ethan asked.

"I've got a favor to ask."

Ethan's hand went to his back pocket. "Yeah?"

A commotion from over by the outdoor stage caught his attention. Jackson Bream was almost running toward a knot of people. Ethan shaded his eyes with his hand... then his chest tightened. Cindy had arrived. Jackson was kissing her cheek.

But the fuss wasn't about Cindy, Ethan realized. Teenage girls swarmed around the taller of the two women flanking her. Then it sank in. These were her sisters, the tall one must be the ex-Miss Georgia. Which meant those two men were her brothers-in-law—the governor would be the one Jackson was fawning over.

Cindy was getting a lot of attention, too, Ethan noted with the kind of proprietary pride he'd only felt—on occasion—for Sam. Everyone wanted to bend her ear about yesterday's judging, all of it positive.

"Can we talk later?" Ethan asked Sam. When he didn't get a reply, he turned to find his son had left. He'd be back, Ethan guessed, if the favor was that important.

As Cindy's party made its way toward him, he drank in the sight of her cute body in those shorts and tank. Her legs were incredible, definitely better than Miss Georgia's.

She was so busy chatting to one of the bonsai growers, she didn't notice Ethan. He saw the moment awareness dawned. Her cheeks turned pink.

Best to get any awkwardness over and done with.

"Good morning, Judge." He took a step toward her.

She stepped backward. "Ethan, hello. I'd like you to meet my sisters, Sabrina and Megan." Her voice was polite, not especially warm. Not surprising. "Girls, this is Ethan Granger. He runs a work program for kids sentenced to community service."

What about, Ethan and I made out last night, he challenged her with his eyes. Then remembered how he'd left. She shot daggers with her gaze.

He lifted his hat to the sisters. He hadn't really noticed Megan, but now he saw she was quite pretty, her hair a darker honey color. She had a nice face, but she didn't have Cindy's instant, eye-catching appeal…though her husband didn't see it that way, judging by the way he watched Ethan as he shook Megan's hand.

Not interested in your wife, buddy. Your sister-in-law, now, she's something else....

After a curt handshake, Ethan turned back to watch the rodeo. Cindy's brothers-in-law found places against the rail, and tucked their respective wives in to watch with them.

A voice called, “Judge Merritt, yoo-hoo!”

Mrs. Baker, of course. She marched toward them. “Judge Merritt,” she said, “I want you to have this.” She thrust a small pink carton at Cindy. “My ginger and hazelnut slice. I think you’ll find it more to your taste than the upside-down cake. Not so sweet.”

“I’m sure I’ll love it.” Cindy had obviously had enough of tasting food in public—she tucked the box into her purse.

Mrs. Baker beamed. “It took guts for you to judge yesterday. None of our male judges has ever been man enough for the job, but you were.”

“Uh, thank you.”

Mrs. Baker’s eyes darted between Ethan and Cindy. “Did you two have a nice evening?” No mistaking the coyness in her tone.

Megan’s head jerked around. She narrowed her gaze on Ethan, who didn’t look away. Then she flicked a glance down at his hands on the rail. A small smile twitched her lips.

Obviously, she realized where he’d left his watch.

Cindy’s brothers-in-law looked to be the protective type. The last thing Ethan needed was some question about his intentions before he even understood what they were himself. Maybe he should hint to Mrs. Baker that the evening hadn't been a date.

"Actually," Cindy said, "we mostly talked about work. Ethan and I don't agree on much, so things don't generally get personal."

Not personal? How the hell did she explain kissing him in the middle of the street?

Mrs. Baker's brow creased.

If Cindy had decided they didn't have anything between them, he was damned if he was going to force the issue. "You know me," he told Mrs. Baker. "I don't do the dating thing seriously."

Cindy glared at him.

"That is a shame," Mrs. Baker said. She left, bemused. Tension crackled between Cindy and Ethan.

"You've changed your tune since last night," he said sourly.

"As soon as the effect of the wine wore off."

He tugged her a few steps away from her sisters. "So, what, if we'd made love you'd be regretting it now?"

"Undoubtedly." She darted a glance at Megan.

"You'd have a smile the size of Texas on your face," he corrected her.

"It would have been a big mistake." She dug into the pocket of her jeans. "Here, this is yours."

His watch. It landed in his hand, warm from its hiding place. It felt as if she was handing back his kisses, the confidences he'd shared with her. The thoughts he'd had this morning about how important she might be in his life. Everything.

He focused hard on his wrist as he slipped the watch on. "Maybe you changed your mind when your sisters arrived with their fancy husbands, and you realized a messed-up rancher wouldn't cut it in your scene."

"You're the one who said we have nothing in common."

Ethan couldn't believe how much that hurt. "So, you admit I was right?"

"It doesn't matter."

And that was before she knew the full truth of his past. How much less would he matter to her then?

Behind them, the PA system crackled. "Would the Youth division saddle bronc competitors please move into the starting area.

Youth division saddle bronc, we need you ready to start."

Ethan grabbed her arm. "We can't leave it—"

"Is that Sam?" Cindy interrupted.

What was his son up to now? Ethan turned and scanned the bleachers.

"There." She pointed. "Next to the ring."

Sam, wearing Ethan's favorite brown Stetson, was one of a dozen young men waiting to ride in the saddle bronc event.

"What the hell? I told him it was too dangerous..." He began elbowing through the crowd, intent on hauling Sam out of the contest, vaguely aware of Cindy following him.

"Our first competitor is Sam Barrett," the announcer said.

Riders competed in alphabetical order in the first round. Ethan cursed.

"Let's have a big hand for Sam, a first-timer today!"

The crowd was generous in its support for a rookie—everyone cheered, from the old granddads in the front row of the bleachers to the toddler held on the rail by his father, waving chubby arms.

Sam was already climbing onto the gray mare in the bucking chute. Eight seconds—

that's how long he had to stay on the horse for his ride to earn points. The mare looked determined to kick him to a bloody pulp. Ethan sped up, but Sam signaled to the chute crew guy that he was ready, and the man opened the gate. The horse burst out and began to buck, the way it had been raised to.

Ethan froze. Through his fear, he noted that Sam had succeeded in marking the mare out. His heels touched the animal's shoulders until its front legs hit the ground. If they hadn't, he'd have been disqualified. Clearly, he'd been practicing. Probably at his friend Dean's house.

It was the longest eight seconds of Ethan's life. And Sam's, going by his white-knuckled grip on the cotton rein attached to the horse's halter. He lifted on the rein, keeping his free hand well clear so he didn't inadvertently make contact with the horse, and tried to find a rhythm, spurring backward and forward with his feet.

Sweat ran down Ethan's back; his palms were dry and hot. His eyes didn't leave his son. Cindy slipped her hand into his. He hung on tight.

When the bell dinged eight seconds, Sam was still on the mare.

"He did it," Cindy said. "Did he win?"

As she spoke, Sam fell from the horse. He rolled out of the horse's way like a pro and jumped to his feet. The horse made a dash for the far end of the arena, eluding both pick-up men, who took off in pursuit.

"He's nowhere near winning," Ethan said roughly. "He stayed on, but he doesn't know the first thing about scoring points."

She punched his arm. "He was great, admit it."

"Maybe." She was right, he couldn't help feeling a burst of pride as he watched Sam head for the fence. Ethan shaded his eyes with his hand, so his pleasure wouldn't be too obvious. Because when he got Sam home he would…what? Tan his hide? Ethan had had enough of that from his stepfather—he wouldn't do it to Sam, even if Sam had been young enough.

He could ground the kid, if he'd listen. For the first time, he felt sympathy for Susan. He couldn't blame her for his son being out of control.

Sam acknowledged the crowd's applause with a jaunty wave. The toddler on the fence wriggled in his dad's grip. His father, distracted by his conversation with his pals, didn't react fast enough—the kid slid over the rail and landed smack in the sawdust. In the path of the bronc and the pick-up man who'd just managed to grab hold of the rein.

A dozen things happened at once. The pick-up man pulled hard on the rein; the bronc showed no interest in stopping. Someone screamed; the kid's dad scrambled over the fence.

And Sam dived for the little boy.

Chapter Thirteen

Sheer insanity, Ethan thought as he vaulted the fence. Sam picked up the boy, flung him at his dad in a lateral pass any quarterback would be proud of. Then he threw his hands over his head to protect himself from the horse. His hat—Ethan's hat—rolled under the hooves. Though the pick-up man had at last gained control of the bronc, one hoof connected with Sam, so fast it was impossible to see where.

The wails of the little boy rose above the ruckus. Ethan knelt by the groaning Sam just as the rodeo doctor reached him.

When Sam struggled to sit up, relief roared

through Ethan like a brush fire. To be followed by a blaze of anger. As soon as he knew his son was okay, he wanted to stick him up against a wall and shake him until his teeth rattled.

"Let me through, I'm the judge." Cindy joined him, the rodeo officials having let her into the ring, uncertain how far her jurisdiction extended.

"Broken wrist," the doctor announced. "We'll get you to the hospital to have it set, son."

Son. He's *my* son, Ethan wanted to say. He'd never actually called Sam that to his face, even though the word haunted his thoughts. Over by the fence, Linnet waited, her knuckles pressed to her mouth. Ethan gave her a sharp nod of reassurance. She turned away; he guessed she was crying.

His eyes met Sam's.

"That was brave," Ethan said. "You saved that child."

Sam ducked his head. "He prob'ly would've been fine."

"He *is* fine, thanks to you." Later, he would figure out how to handle Sam's defiance in entering the damn rodeo in the first place.

"Let's get you to the hospital." He helped

Sam to his feet. His son's shoulders were bony, his arms muscled. His hair was full of sawdust and grit and he was the handsomest kid Ethan had ever seen.

Linnet met them at the gate. "Sam, honey. Oh, Sam." She hugged him carefully; Sam hugged back.

Ethan heard worried female voices. "Your sisters," he reminded Cindy. She glanced over her shoulder, then back at Ethan.

"I could come to the hospital with you," she said.

He could have kissed her.

"Come see us later," he said. "When you're free."

Cynthia's family stayed until late afternoon, lingering over the lunch they'd brought with them, prepared by Sabrina, a *Cordon Bleu* cook, and transported from Atlanta.

At five, the visitors announced their intention of heading back to the city. Cynthia embraced Jake, then Sabrina. "Drive safely."

"We always do," Sabrina said. She was paranoid about road safety. "It's been great seeing your new life. I can't believe how many people you know—you really seem to be a part of the town."

Cynthia smiled. "Thanks. Tell Dad that, would you?"

"Sure." Sabrina looked puzzled. She'd never fully understood that Jonah loved her differently from the way he loved Cynthia and Megan. He loved Sabrina unconditionally.

Cynthia shared a glance with Megan as she hugged her middle sister. Sabrina didn't have a malicious bone in her body, so there was no point telling her how things were.

"Good luck with Ethan," Megan whispered.

Cynthia's stomach plummeted. She wasn't about to beg Megan not to tell Dad she'd gotten involved with a man here. But it would be very convenient if Megan failed to mention it.

When Cynthia arrived in the emergency room, Ethan was reading the newspaper beside Sam's bed; Sam was staring at the ceiling.

The E.R. was busy, mostly with injuries from the fair, a nurse had told her, so Sam didn't notice Cynthia until she'd almost reached his bedside.

"How are you feeling?" She handed over several packets of chocolate—Milk Duds and

Peanut Butter Cups. She'd called Ethan on his cell and he'd told her those were Sam's favorites.

"Okay." He dumped them on the nightstand. "Thanks for the gift."

Ethan stood and gave her his chair. "Thanks for coming by."

"My pleasure." He looked tired. She wanted to hold him. "You okay?"

"Aside from out of my mind with worry about this dude." He nodded at Sam.

"You were great today, Sam," Cynthia said. "The way you reacted, saving that boy by putting yourself in harm's way, says a lot about your character."

"Cynthia's right," Ethan agreed. "I'm proud of you."

Sam eyeballed his dad. As was often the case, he seemed to be waiting for more. Something niggled at Cynthia, but she couldn't place it. Then Sam closed his eyes. His face was pale.

"Did they give you painkillers?" she asked.

He grunted. "Not sure they're working."

"The nurse is bringing a supply for us to take away, and we're waiting for the doc to clear us to leave," Ethan said. "Then we'll go back to the Double T."

Sam turned his head to one side. Cynthia thought she caught a glimpse of tears. "Sam, are you all right?" Oops, that was probably the worst thing to do, draw attention to it.

Sure enough…

"I friggin' broke my wrist," he snarled. "It hurts, okay?"

"I bet your mom was worried."

His jaw jutted. "She hasn't called back yet."

Oh, help.

The attending physician showed up before Cynthia could make things worse. "You ready to go home, Sam?"

"Where's that?" Sam muttered.

"Just sign him out and we'll give you back your bed," Ethan said.

The doctor scrawled something on a clipboard. "The nurse will have you fixed up with painkillers, then you're free to leave."

"Thanks." Ethan turned to Cynthia. "You want to come back with us, have some dinner?" He caught her fingers in his.

"Another day," she said. "You and Sam need some time together." She read something in Sam's eyes, longing and fear. Fear of what? Again she had that niggling feeling, a kind of recognition. But she couldn't pin it down. And no matter what Ethan said about the anger he'd felt in his troubled youth, he would never physically harm his son.

"Can I have a word with you while Sam waits for the nurse?" she asked Ethan. She hadn't come here only to see Sam. She'd spent most of today thinking about where things stood with Ethan.

He followed her out into the corridor. Cynthia checked him out, sidelong. He looked lean and strong and kind. The kind of man a girl—a woman—could depend on. But as he'd said about the cakes, appearances could be deceptive.

He laced his fingers through hers. "Thanks for offering to leave your family and come with me today."

"That's okay."

He tugged her into an alcove that housed a couple of vending machines. "I'm sorry I accused you of not wanting anything with me because your family moves in bigger circles. I was out of line."

Somehow they'd ended up standing almost touching. Cynthia's plan to remind him they'd reached a stalemate last night and maybe they should settle for that flew out the window.

"Mmm," she said, anticipating.

"Mmm," he agreed and kissed her. His tongue brushed her lips and she let him in.

Time stood still as they kissed, not groping each other, since they were in a public place, but with a sweet languor that seeped through every cell in Cynthia's body.

"Howdy, y'all." The sheriff's voice jerked her back to consciousness.

As Ethan straightened, Cynthia tugged at her tank top, which had ridden up.

"Good to see you, Judge." Sheriff Davis sounded highly amused.

"You, too, Sheriff."

"Just come to take a statement from your boy," the sheriff told Ethan.

Ethan took a step forward. "He saved a child, surely he can't be in trouble."

"Routine accident report," the sheriff assured him. "No trouble at all. I won't be more than ten minutes, if you two want to keep, uh, talking."

Cynthia narrowed her eyes. He grinned and sauntered into the E.R.

"The whole town will know we were kissing again by suppertime," Ethan observed.

Cynthia groaned.

"Is that a problem?" he said coolly.

She pressed the Coke button on the vending

machine as an excuse not to meet his eyes. “I told you what I want in a relationship—the level of emotional security I need. It didn’t sound like what you wanted to give.” And now she was a hot prospect for the judgeship in Atlanta, so it might not even be relevant.

He stepped closer, forcing her to look up. “We had one date. Isn’t that a bit early to decide how far it’s going to go?”

“I like you a lot, Ethan. More than I can remember liking anyone in a long while.”

His head jerked back.

“See?” she said. “I scared you.”

“You didn’t *scare* me.” He folded his arms and stared her down. “But do you have to always say exactly what you’re thinking? Couldn’t you wait until maybe I’m ready to hear it?”

“No,” she said. A nurse going past turned at Cynthia’s sharp tone. She lowered her voice. “I don’t want to get distracted by thoughts of a relationship with you that in all likelihood would be a disaster, when I should be thinking about getting back to my family.”

She slipped by him, out into the corridor, removing the privacy from the conversation.

“So that’s it,” he said, “we’re not dating because you think I’m never going to be able to give you the emotional commitment you want, and you're not willing to wait and see."

She felt as if she was letting go of something very precious...something too hard to hold. She spread her fingers at her sides. "That's it," she agreed.

Linnet perused Hollow Hardware's range of tape measures. Ethan was impossible to buy for, but she couldn't ignore his birthday. Not without sending a message she didn't intend. Not when they were finally making some progress, thanks to Cynthia.

She started down aisle five. Safety, Security, Flashlights.

Everyone needed a flashlight—the old ones always broke. Not the most meaningful gift. Did it say, *Don't keep me in the dark, son?* She smiled to herself. It would certainly be apt.

Linnet wondered if Cynthia knew it was Ethan's birthday next month. Mind you, the judge would probably make a choice in five minutes. It always took Linnet weeks of anxious browsing, and she was never satisfied with her decision. Rather like her life.

Linnet wasn't crazy about Cynthia, but she figured the judge might grow on her. And

Ethan sure needed someone strong like that, a woman who wouldn't let herself be stymied by his refusal to engage.

"Hi, Gram." Sam appeared at the end of the aisle.

"Sam, honey." Her smile widened. What a treasure to have a grandchild. She might have known she wouldn't end up with one of those easy ones, like Jackie Browne's angelic choirboy grandson. She didn't care. However difficult Sam was, he was a part of her. Always would be. "What are you doing here?"

"Al has me running errands, because of this." He held up his injured arm, in a cast and a sling.

"I'm hunting for something for your dad's birthday. Did you know it's August first?"

Sam scowled. "That's ages away."

"To you, maybe." Linnet wondered if Ethan had gotten mad about the rodeo. Probably not—he would have had another of those reasonable discussions that got Sam so riled up. She sighed and picked up a super heavy-duty flashlight. "August feels like tomorrow to me. Do you think he'd like this?"

Sam shrugged.

Linnet returned the light to the shelf. "How's your wrist?"

"No pain, just a pain in the butt." The cast explained why he was wearing an old plaid shirt of Ethan's rather than one of his ubiquitous black T-shirts. The plaid suited him. Softened him.

"What's happening with your community service in the park?" Linnet asked. Sam had been assigned to planting, but that would be impractical with his injury.

"I'm on litter detail." A sneer told her what he thought of that.

"Judge Merritt been out to your place recently?" Did he know the sheriff had walked in on Ethan and Cynthia in a clinch? Hot stuff, by all accounts. She presumed that was why they hadn't been seen together the past few days. But it took more than lying low to dampen a rumor around this town. Especially after they'd kissed outside Sally's.

Sam picked up a flashlight, a Maglite, and read the packaging. "Haven't seen her."

"That's the most powerful light for its size." Linnet had read the packaging, too. "Maybe I should check out the screwdriver sets. I gave your dad one of those when he was twelve years old." She wondered what message a screwdriver set would send. *You screwed me up, Mom.* Or was that *screwed me over?* Linnet rubbed her forehead. She had to accept Ethan for who he was, if she ever wanted him to do the same for her. She pulled a fire blanket down from a higher shelf. Every home should have one. *You smothered me?* No, he could never accuse her of that.

"My mom never called," Sam said suddenly. "After I broke my wrist. Dad phoned to tell her I was in the hospital, and she said she'd call me but she never did."

"Honey, I'm sorry." Linnet put the blanket back on the shelf. "She's probably working long hours and can't get—"

"My mom once told me you threw my dad out when he was my age. Did you?"

Her hands fluttered at her sides. "I don't know what you're talking about," she said automatically.

That wasn't going to work this time.

"Did you throw him out?" Sam demanded.

"I—he was in a lot of trouble, Sam. I couldn't deal with it."

He flipped the Maglite flashlight between his fingers, urgent, agitated. "Dad told me he did some stupid stuff. He didn't tell me what."

Linnet's hands flapped. "It's not for me to say. Your father—he didn't get along with Wayne, my husband."

"So you threw out your son and kept your husband?"

A deep, inner shame broke out of the place deep inside where she kept it locked away. "Honey, these things aren't simple."

"Forget it." He tossed the flashlight in the air. Just when she thought he would drop it and she would have to pay for it, he caught it.

"I hate to argue with you." A headache pulsed behind her eyes. "I'll get your dad's present another day." She turned her back on the shelves laden with potential mistakes. "How about you finish your errand, then we go to my place for some—" She stopped, cold to the marrow.

"Some what?" Sam asked.

Linnet swallowed, tried to keep her gaze on his face while she checked out what she'd seen in her peripheral vision. *There.* Inside the concealing folds of Sam's sling, she glimpsed the edge of the Maglite packaging.

"Gram? You okay?" He had no idea she'd noticed.

Her teeth chattered; she bit down. What to do? She and Sam…he was so good with her, they got along so well, apart from the argument they'd had just now. Stealing the flashlight was probably a reaction to that—it was practically her fault.

If she confronted him, Sam would be angry. Angri*er.* He'd make a fuss and they would attract attention. Miles Drake, the store owner, would hear and have Sam arrested. Even if he didn't, she and Sam would both know she couldn't trust him anymore. What then?

"Some tea," she murmured, finishing her original sentence. *I can't let him get away with it. It's stealing. Dear God, he's getting worse. What should I do?* She wanted to help Sam—getting him into more trouble wouldn't help. *Neither will letting him become a thief.*

He was Ethan's son. Ethan's problem. She would let Sam go, then she would phone Ethan and tell him what happened. He could deal with it.

She'd let Ethan deal with that other mess, all those years ago, hadn't she?

"Tea sounds good." Sam's eyes were bright with adrenaline, with the high of gambling he could get away with his crime. "Let's go."

He started down the aisle, his arm held close to his torso as if it hurt. Wouldn't want to dislodge his loot.

Linnet wrung her hands. *It's not my responsibility.*

What exactly was your role in my upbringing, Mom? She remembered the bitter question from Ethan when she'd first shown up in Stonewall Hollow and told him they were family so it was good to live in the same place. It had hurt at the time, a searing pain with the sting of truth in its tail. Because she hadn't done all she could for Ethan. All she should have. She hadn't wanted to rock her fragile, patched-up, second-rate marriage.

Wayne had done wrong, and she'd let him. Let him order her around, disrespect her, be tougher on Ethan than he had any right to be. Then Ethan had done wrong, and she'd turned a blind eye, on the complicit assumption that anything was permissible, so long as Wayne didn't find out. That was all she wanted to know back then: Would Wayne find out? She'd told herself she was giving Ethan the freedom he apparently craved, while preserving the stability of life at home.

I'm a coward.

"Sam," she called, her voice low and scratchy. Guilt must have sharpened his hearing. He slowed. "Put it back."

He stopped. Turned. "Huh?"

"The flashlight. Put it back."

His face flushed. "Whaddya mean?"

She might not know much about being a good parent, but she knew all about teenage boys and circuitous arguments that went nowhere. She said nothing, just stared at him.

"It's for Dad," Sam said. "For his birthday."

Linnet wanted to weep. "You'd do that to your father? Something you know he'll find so repugnant, and call it a gift?"

He shrugged.

A surge of protectiveness toward Ethan stiffened her backbone. Yes, she knew it was too little and too late, but it was the same instinct that had provoked her dislike of Cynthia, when she had refused to sentence Sam the way Ethan wanted. "I'll report you."

He snorted. "Sure you will. Come on, Gram, let's go have that tea. You can give me a lecture if you want." He flashed her a charming smile that put her in mind of Ethan's father. Who'd been a decent enough young man, but who'd never faced up to his responsibilities and had allowed his parents to provide what they could for Linnet and her baby. One thing about Ethan, he faced up to his responsibilities and then some. Who knew where he got that?

Linnet forced one foot in front of the other.

When she reached Sam, she grabbed his injured arm.

"Ow, Gram!" He wrenched away from her.

"Put. It. Back."

"It's a friggin' twenty-dollar flashlight." He strode away, his walk just like Ethan's as he headed for the main doors. No electronic alarms in this store, which he doubtless had checked before he started thieving.

Linnet's mouth filled with saliva, her eyes with tears; it was as if something inside her was dissolving. Half-blind, she made her way to the customer service desk.

"Excuse me," she said to the assistant. "That young man—he stole a flashlight. It's in his sling."

As the man radioed Miles Drake, who moved swiftly to stop Sam, Linnet pressed her knuckles against her teeth and prayed that doing the right thing for someone she loved would feel good.

It didn't.

Chapter Fourteen

Ethan's cell phone rang as he wrestled with a hay wrapper stuck on the baler. "Can you see who it is?" he asked Connor, still working off the cost of that oil he'd spilled.

Connor leaned over to check the phone clipped to Ethan's belt. "Mom," he read with a grin. "Yours, I guess."

Ethan grimaced. He didn't want to talk to his mother. He hadn't felt like talking to anyone much since Cindy had blown him off. But Linnet didn't call without a reason. The ringing stopped, and a minute later he heard a beep to say he had a message. When he'd freed the wrapper, he called her.

"Oh... Ethan." She was jittery, quick little breaths coming over the airwaves.

"Didn't you just call?"

"Yes, I, um, left a message." She half sounded as if she didn't want to speak to him.

"What is it?" he said brusquely.

"Sam's been arrested," she blurted. "For shoplifting."

The four-letter word he barked made the kids snigger. He didn't normally swear in front of them.

Linnet filled him in. Sam had stolen a flashlight from the hardware store. Stashed it in his sling—the badge of his heroism—of all places. They'd let him walk out the door, then nabbed him.

"I asked Miles not to press charges," Linnet said.

"You were there?" Ethan's picture of events shifted, changed.

"But he said if he lets one kid get away with it, they'll all have a go."

"You were there?" he asked again. "Couldn't you have stopped him, dammit? Didn't you see?"

The silence was so complete, he thought they'd been cut off. He shook the phone. "Mom?"

"I tried to stop him," she said. "He wouldn't listen."

Damn stubborn kid. "Thanks," he said grudgingly. "I guess you did your best." Just because he and Cindy had nothing going, didn't mean he shouldn't stick to the truce she'd inspired.

"Ethan." Linnet's voice was almost a squeak. "It was me who reported Sam for stealing."

"What the—" He stumbled backward, almost fell over one of the kids, who'd sprawled on the grass while they waited. The need to count to ten came upon him like never before. Twice. Three times. He barked the numbers in his head.

"Ethan? Are you still there?"

"You didn't just say—"

"What was I supposed to do?" she demanded, feistier than he'd ever heard her. "Let him think it's okay to steal?"

She'd turned a blind eye when Ethan did it. "You picked a fine time to learn how to be a parent," he growled.

"Shut up, Ethan."

He looked at the phone.

"You need to come in and get Sam from the station," she said. "If you don't want to, I can deal with it."

"I'll come," he said sharply. "I'm not going to give up on *my* son."

He heard a gasp from Linnet, but she refrained from one of her digs. Ethan felt ashamed that he'd stooped to her kind of tactic. But not that ashamed.

On the way into town, he phoned Cindy. Whichever way he looked at it, it was the wrong thing to do—calling her because she was the judge was one of those conflicts of interest she got so het up about, and she wasn't his girlfriend.

But her voice…just hearing it lifted some weight off his shoulders. Despite what she'd said the other day, she sounded pretty happy to hear from him, too, her voice warm. Until she heard why he was calling.

"What did he steal?" she asked, as soon as he finished explaining.

"I don't know." Then he remembered. "A flashlight."

"So it must be worth less than three hundred dollars."

"What does that have to do with it?"

"That's the point at which Georgia law deems shoplifting a felony, rather than a misdemeanor."

A felony. *Hell.* A superior court trial, possible jail sentence. Ethan knew a wild gratitude that his son hadn't been able to fit a chain saw in his sling.

"My mother called the cops on Sam." He told her what had happened.

"Poor Linnet," Cindy said, "what an awful position to be in."

"Poor her?" Ethan said, incredulous. "Why didn't she just tell me?"

"Would you have let Sam get away with stealing?"

"Of course not."

"Then what does it matter?"

"It matters," Ethan said. It mattered because Linnet had never stood by him, and now she'd let go of Sam, too, even if it was the right thing to do. He knew his logic didn't add up, but he wasn't in a frame of mind to give his mother the benefit of the doubt. "So if shoplifting's a misdemeanor," he said, "Sam will appear before you?"

Cindy's sigh said it all.

Ethan slowed for a bend in the road. "I'm not asking for special treatment."

"Just as well," she said sharply. "I'll transfer the case to Gonville. I mean, I know you and I aren't seeing each other…."

Was that an expectant pause?

"I miss you," he said, before he could think better of it. He found himself holding his breath.

"I miss you, too."

Elation surged through him. "I might have been too quick to say you and I wouldn't work out."

"Mmm," she said noncommittally.

This felt oddly like some of his conversations with Sam. Uncertain. Floundering.

Only Sam was ruder.

"I want to give us a chance," he said, "to see if we can make sense of this. Please?" His voice had gone disturbingly high. He cleared his throat.

He heard a soft laugh down the line. "You've got it."

Three simple words.

Cynthia tried to focus on the facts being presented in the civil case she was hearing. She shouldn't feel so happy, not when Sam was in trouble, and Ethan still hadn't managed to put two emotional words together. Besides, she hadn't dared think about having to choose between a life spent following her heart, or one spent chasing her father's love.

Between a man—who might, for example, be Ethan—and the superior court. But Ethan had said he wanted to try, and it seemed that was enough to produce a ridiculous amount of optimism in her.

"Sustained," she said in response to one of the lawyer's objections. The case was a breach of contract, so minor she wanted to tell the interested parties to go home and get a life, but she was trying to be more tactful these days.

She referred to the exhibit the bailiff handed her, a schedule of loan repayments. The numbers didn't keep her attention.

Meeting Ethan had forced her to hold a lamp up to her relationship with her dad, and she hadn't liked what she saw. In her heart, she didn't believe her father loved her only if she was meeting his expectations in her work. She didn't want to live with that feeling that she could only be loved if she was good enough. That she wasn't loved as much as she loved.

Should she ever have kids of her own, she would make sure they knew they were loved exactly as they were.

The way Ethan loved Sam, if only Sam—

If only Sam could see it.

Those niggling feelings she'd had about Sam suddenly came into focus. Sam had no idea Ethan loved him!

Ethan had told Cynthia he loved Sam, under duress, but had he ever said those words to his son? He guarded his emotions so carefully with the boy…would Sam be in the trouble he was in now, if he recognized how precious he was to his father? Or was he trying to provoke some kind of emotional response—*any* kind of emotion—from his father?

He was the opposite of Cynthia, whose attempts to win her father's love involved complying, being the person her dad wanted. Sam went the other way, putting his father's love to the test, looking for proof.

Someone ought to tell Sam how Ethan felt.

Ideally, that someone should be Ethan. But how likely was that to happen, with Sam's latest arrest?

Maybe someone else should do it. Like her.

No way! She barely knew Sam, she was the judge who'd sentenced him.

Cynthia tried to chase the thought away, but couldn't she of all people understand how it felt to have a father who didn't readily show his love. And she'd at least had the security of knowing Jonah always wanted her in his life, even if his feelings weren't as unconditional as she'd like. Poor Sam…

Having finished presenting his evidence, the lawyer sat down. The clerk turned to Cynthia. "Almost noon, Your Honor."

"We'll take a two-hour recess," she announced.

Cynthia found Sam picking up litter around the kids' playground at Stonewall Gardens.

"I don't have to listen to you," he said as soon as she got within reach. "We're not in court."

"No, and you won't be in my court, either. I'm going to ask the clerk to send your case over to Gonville."

He paled. "But—still in the state court, right?"

It always amazed her how much the kids who got into trouble knew about the legal system. She nodded. "I'm transferring you because I might have a personal interest in the case."

"I don't want to hear about you and my dad." He picked up a Sprite can, crushed it in his palm and threw it in the trash.

Too bad. "I'm here to tell you what your father's not saying."

He snorted, he scuffed the grass with his foot.

"Let's go sit in my car for a few minutes," she said. "The air-conditioning's on, it's nicely chilled." It had to be nearly a hundred out here, and humid as anything.

The appeal of getting out of the sun swung Sam's cooperation. He pulled off his work glove with his teeth and stuffed it in his pocket.

In the car, Cynthia turned up the air, then twisted to face him. "Sam, I had to come. I just realized you have no idea how your father feels about you."

"What the—" He put his hand on the door handle.

"You don't realize how much he loves you."

Sam flinched. "What is this?"

"The truth," she said. "Your father is making a total hash of it, but he loves you so much, just looking at you gets him all choked up."

As he made to open the door, Cynthia hit the central lock.

"Hey!" He half lunged toward her, before he got himself under control.

"If he could hold you in his arms and tell you he loves you—"

"He'd better not try." Sam's voice cracked. "Let me out of here, this is abduction."

With a good enough lawyer, he was right.

Cynthia quashed her alarm. She couldn't stop now. "Ethan's afraid to admit the depth of his feelings. Not just to you, to everyone. He's bottled his emotions for so many years, he's scared that if he lets them out—"

"Telling me this crap isn't going to *fix* me," Sam said. "I know what I am to Ethan, and that's just one more problem kid, like all the other problem kids."

Cynthia balled her fists in frustration. "He's crazy about you. He told me he loved you the instant he heard you existed."

His brows drew together.

"It's true," she insisted. "Sam, your dad can be dumb about showing it..."

"He's not dumb," he said, and for a moment she thought he was defending his father. Then he added, "He knows exactly what he's showing me. Dumb people don't have law degrees."

"He doesn't—" Cynthia stopped. "Ethan has a law degree?"

"Yeah," Sam said impatiently. "Which means he's not dumb, so you're wrong. The reason he can't show he cares is because he doesn't."

She set aside her curiosity about Ethan's education. "He told me he hates the way he's messing up with you. That he wants to get to know you—you should have seen the longing in his face."

She caught the same longing in Sam's face. For one second, before he wiped it. "Why are you saying all this?" he asked.

"Your dad won't be happy until he puts things right with you, and the same goes for you. Give him a chance, Sam, to show you his love," Cynthia said. "It's tough, but someone has to go first. Open up to him and you won't regret it."

"Why? So you and him and me can be one big happy family?"

So. He'd heard the gossip. She ran a hand over her face. "Sam, the only time I'm a hundred percent sure my dad loves me is when I'm getting something right that matters to him."

He stilled.

"Even then Dad never really shows me he loves me. I hate that," she said. "I want to be certain he loves me all the time, just for who I am. You have the chance to know that about your father. Take it."

He stared at her. Then he blinked rapidly. He cursed and slammed his palm against the window. "Open up, or I'm calling the cops."

She'd said what she'd intended, so she let him out. He stomped away without looking back. Had she got through?

Cynthia started the engine. As she drove, she mulled over Ethan's alleged law degree. Why hadn't he told her? His qualifications didn't make him any more appealing to her, of course. She already thought he was incredible. But her father would like him better for it.

She imagined Ethan sitting down with her dad and Megan, talking about some case that was in the headlines. In her scenario, every so often he would reach across the table and squeeze her hand. There would be such tenderness in Ethan's eyes that Megan would sigh and say, "No wonder you love him."

She screeched to a halt at a red light, drawing a friendly wave from a pedestrian. "I don't love Ethan," she said aloud.

Yes, I do. The knowledge hit her heart and mind simultaneously. She'd fallen in love with him, without even noticing.

The light turned green and she inched forward, automatically returning a salute from Jackson Bream.

"This is silly," she muttered. Okay, so Ethan understood her, admired the woman beneath the judge's surface. He made her feel desired and cherished for the way she was, not for her career potential. She was pretty sure he wouldn't think any less of her if she decided to be something other than a judge.

Then there was his determination, albeit misguided, to make amends for the past and reconcile his family.

She groaned. Who wouldn't love that?

And now that she'd admitted it, what the heck was she supposed to do about it? How was she supposed to just walk away from him and from Stonewall Hollow if they couldn't iron out the differences between them?

What if he doesn't love me back?

She would go see Ethan tomorrow.... No! Tomorrow, Justice Pearson would be here. Cynthia flicked her turn signal and drove into the courthouse parking lot. She pulled into the parking space marked Judge and turned the engine off.

She had to go ahead with her interview with Justice Pearson. If things didn't work out with Ethan...it was all very well saying she didn't want her old life back, but where would that leave her.

Cynthia opened her door. She would go see Ethan tonight.

I'll tell him about my talk with Sam. She would make Ethan see how critical it was that he open up to his son—and to her. She would make it happen.

Tonight.

Ethan called Cynthia before she could call him, which she took as an excellent sign.

"Come for dinner," he said. "Sam's out with his buddies, it'll be just you and me. I'd like us to talk."

"About anything in particular?"

"Just, you know, sharing stuff," he muttered.

She found herself beaming into the phone. "Stuff being feelings?"

"I guess."

"An offer I can't refuse," she said brightly, and was pretty sure he groaned.

She was singing under her breath as she got ready to go out and drove to the Double T. She was once again wearing the yellow sundress, which she was now sick of the sight of. Tomorrow she would go online and order a new dress.

No, tomorrow Justice Pearson would be here. Everything else would have to wait.

She'd better tell Ethan about the justice, along with all the other things she had to say.

"You look amazing, as always." Ethan greeted her with a kiss that soon grew seriously hot.

"Mmm." That low, humming sound came from somewhere deep within her. His kiss was sweet temptation of a kind she'd never known.

At last, he released her. "If we're going to eat, I'd better get some self-control."

"I guess." Her appetite had disappeared but they still had all that talking to do.

He poured them both a glass of red wine, then pulled a bowl of chicken pieces sitting in some kind of milky mixture from the fridge. "Fried chicken," he said. "My housekeeper prepared it, all we need to do is cook it."

"You mean, deep-fry it?"

"As long as the oil's the right temperature, so it doesn't get absorbed, this is practically health food," he assured her.

She raised her glass to him.

When he dropped the pieces in a pan of hot oil, they sizzled and spat.

"It's important not to walk away at this stage," he said. "That's how you burn the house down. Think you could set the table for me?"

"Hey, I have a Harvard law degree, magna cum laude." That wasn't subtle, but she was dying to know the truth about Ethan's degree.

"You're eminently qualified to set tables," he approved.

"How about you?" she said. "What's your qualification to fry that chicken?"

"I've been doing it once a week for ten years."

Rats. She pulled knives and forks from the drawer he indicated. "Did you ever get to college?"

He used a slotted spoon to separate two pieces of chicken that were trying to stick together in the bubbling fat. He said nothing for so long, she started to think about how she could rephrase the question without being too obvious.

Then he said slowly, "Matter of fact, I did a criminal justice degree."

"Really?" Sam hadn't had it quite right, but it was almost as good as a law degree. "Which school?"

"Ohio University. They have a great distance-learning program."

Not Ivy League, but who cared? "Did you ever use your degree in your work?"

He shook his head. "I met Paul Siddons right after I graduated and he offered me a job out here. We just clicked, I was keen to work with him."

His lack of a father figure might have something to do with that, Cynthia suspected. "But I suppose your studies gave you your passion for youth offenders."

"I told you, I used to be a bad kid." He removed a piece of chicken with a slotted spoon and set it to drain on a paper towel. Then he went back in for another one. It was careful work, with the fat still spitting; he didn't look at her. "I was worse than you imagine."

"You don't know what I imagine." That came out way more seductive than she intended.

His eyes darkened, a smile curved his mouth. "Are you deliberately saying that when I can't do anything about it?" He removed the pan from the stove. "Give me one minute and you'll have my full attention."

"I can just about wait one minute," she said happily.

They heard tires on gravel outside. Ethan groaned.

“Is it Sam?” she asked.

He shook his head. “It’s not the Mazda. Sounds like the sheriff’s cruiser. He lives out this way. Can you get the door while I wash my hands?”

“Gee, am I interrupting something again?” Sheriff Davis’s raspy voice bore unmistakable amusement when she opened the door.

“Come on in.” Cynthia led the way to the kitchen.

“Beer, Mike?” Ethan asked.

The sheriff fingered the brim of his hat. “I’m here on business. I should have phoned but my shift just ended—thought I’d stop by on my way home.” All trace of humor had vanished; he sounded quiet and serious.

Ethan put the chicken in the oven to keep warm. “Is there a problem?”

The sheriff put his hat on the table. “Sam’s been arrested again.”

Ethan swore; Cynthia gasped.

“More shoplifting?” Ethan asked.

He sounded almost hopeful, and Cynthia could guess why. Young offenders tended to escalate their crimes, not do the same thing again. *Not armed robbery, please.*

“Arson,” the sheriff said grimly. “Or, lucky

for him, attempted arson," he amended. "We caught him just in time."

"So he's been charged with...?" Cynthia asked.

"Criminal trespass," the sheriff said. "He was found in back of the community hall in possession of an accelerant, a lighter, some rags and papers."

"Unlawful purpose." She sighed.

"In this weather, a fire would be out of control in no time," Ethan said grimly.

The sheriff nodded. "Bill Lavender's on duty, if you want to go pick Sam up."

"I'll go now." Ethan grabbed his jacket, slung over a chair at the kitchen table. Cynthia picked up her purse.

"You're coming, too?" Ethan asked.

"Of course." And not just for Ethan's sake. She hurried outside with him, shivering although it was still warm. Had her visit to Sam in some way triggered his latest rampage? Would he tell Ethan it had, whether that was true or not? She picked up her pace.

"We'll take my car," she suggested to Ethan. "It's best not to drive when you're upset."

"I'm not upset," Ethan said. "I'm just going to kill him."

The sheriff nodded his approval.

"You can bring Sam's car home," she reminded him.

Cynthia needed to tell Ethan she'd visited Sam.... She shuddered at the thought of the hall burning down.

In the Volvo, they started down the long driveway. "Ethan, about Sam..."

"I'm glad you're with me," he said, as he buckled his seat belt. "It feels right." He reached over and squeezed her hand on the wheel.

She managed a halfhearted smile. Would it feel so right when she told Ethan Sam had apparently decided to burn down the hall right after her little chat with him?

Maybe he didn't need to add that to his pile of worries just now.

Chapter Fifteen

Huddled in the corner of a police cell, Sam looked far younger than his eighteen years. When he saw Ethan, tears started to his eyes. "Dad." He came over to the bars.

Cynthia wondered if he'd been this emotional after his previous arrests.

Ethan didn't smile but his face was relaxed. She couldn't imagine how he achieved such serenity. Resentment glimmered in Sam's expression.

"You've messed up, Sam," Ethan said, his voice way too even for a dad whose son was a match-strike away from a prison sentence. "When you're done with the legal process, we're going to have to make some changes. I can't stand by and let you destroy your life."

Sam wrapped his fingers around the cell bars. "You're throwing me out?"

"I'm getting you some counseling, which you will attend if you want to eat in my house." He glanced at Cynthia, as if she would be pleased. That's right, she'd expressed concern when they met that Ethan didn't hook up with any counseling programs. But now, she knew exactly what Sam needed, and it wasn't another stranger to talk to.

"Screw you," Sam said.

Ethan's lips tightened. The door from reception opened and Sam's lawyer, Tom Cadman, walked in.

Cadman had appeared before her several times; she rated him the best in town. She nodded reassurance to Sam, but was reluctant to draw attention to herself in case he mentioned their little "abduction" episode. She would confess to Ethan tonight. It would sound better coming from her.

"I don't need to tell you, this is serious." Tom eyed her.

"It's likely the case will be heard in Gonville," she said. "But if it makes you more comfortable, I'll leave."

Out in the office, Deputy Lavender was making coffee. "Bad business," he said, with a nod toward the cells. "The kid's in court tomorrow on that shoplifting charge. The D.A. will probably tack this escapade on, too."

"Hmm." He didn't need to know Cynthia would be telling the D.A. to take his case elsewhere.

Hopefully without alerting Justice Pearson to the fact she was in love with the father of one of her defendants.

It was ten o'clock by the time Cynthia and Ethan walked out into the parking lot. Not late, but she was exhausted. Ethan was, too, she could tell from the lines beneath his eyes. Sam had refused to come home. He planned to stay the night at his friend Dean's house. Since he was eighteen, his dad couldn't force him to return to the ranch.

Ethan's shoulders were rigid. "The sooner I get Sam into some serious counseling, the better."

"If you send Sam to a counselor, he'll see it as another rejection," she warned.

He stopped halfway to her car. "What do you mean *another* rejection? And you're the one who was gung ho about counseling."

"I've changed my mind," she said. "Sam's been rejected by his mom, he came here looking for love."

"I love him," he said impatiently.

"*I* know it, but he doesn't," she said. "How would he? What do people do when they love someone, Ethan? They tell them, they hug them, and most of all they get mad at them—no one makes you madder than the people you love. Sam commits crimes to get your attention and you stand there so calm and considered, as if he's some kid who's not related to you. Like his lawyer! I'll bet you've never told Sam how mad he makes you, let alone how much you love him."

She was raving, but from his recoil, she guessed she was right. "It's the same with your mom," she said. "You both have all this resentment toward each other, but you won't have a stand-up fight about it."

"Leave Linnet out of this."

"The kids in your program don't need you to love them," she continued. "But Sam...why do you think he's still here in town, when he could be making his way in the world, the way you were at his age? He's not lazy, and he makes good money at Al's."

"How would I know why he's still here?"

Ethan stalked away. The orange light from the streetlamp fell on his face, accentuating harsh planes.

"He's still here on the chance that one day you'll love him. The same with your mom—she's been hanging around for years." The same reason Cynthia was still jumping to do whatever her father wanted. She wanted to warn Ethan she'd had enough hanging around waiting to be loved, that she wouldn't be prepared to do the same with him, but now wasn't the time.

"Ethan, you're not an angry teenager who might snap at any moment. If you want a future with Sam, with your mom...with a woman...you have to give your heart. You can't make headway with Sam until you stop looking at him as a troubled kid who needs guidance, and just see him as the infuriating son you love."

She didn't have to see him to know his expression would have closed up. She was asking for way more honesty than he thought he could reveal.

"Are you going to unlock this car?" he asked.

She didn't budge. "I know about dads who withhold affection, or seem to, for whatever reason. It hurts. Sam needs to believe you love him no matter what. He told me today he doesn't think you love him at all."

He wheeled around. "Today?"

Damn. "I went to see him at the park at lunchtime," she said. "I realized he needed to know how you felt, and I understand you wouldn't tell him." When she said it aloud, she understood she'd taken a terrible liberty.

"You went to see him...and then he went straight out and tried to start a fire?" Ethan's voice was dangerously quiet.

She swallowed. "He didn't seem upset, but of course I have to consider that I might have—"

"You have way overstepped the mark." Fury welled inside Ethan, exacerbating the raw nerve Cindy's words had struck. He'd spent years making sure he wasn't the guy he used to be, and now she was saying he'd got it all wrong! "I love my son, and he's smart enough to figure that out. He certainly doesn't need you feeding him your variety of psychobabble."

"If you think you can express your emotions," she said, "I dare you to tell me right now what you feel for me."

"What?" Where did that come from? How could he distinguish what he felt for her, with everything else going on?

"Because I can tell you what I feel for you." She drew a long breath. "When I'm with you, I get a glimpse of what my sisters have with their husbands. I get a glimpse of forever."

His heart pounded. Did she mean that?

"See, it's easy," she said. "Your turn."

He swallowed. He could do this. Mad though he was about Sam, he could do this. "You're beautiful," he said. "And smart."

"Stop, you're killing me."

He paced beneath the streetlamp. "Right, you want feelings? Here they are. I like talking to you, you make me laugh. You're so forthright, and that takes a lot of courage. You stand by your opinions until the last possible moment, then you're not afraid to say you made a mistake. You have a great attitude to family, you'd make a great mom—"

"Stop!" She held up a hand. "Don't recite a shopping list of my good qualities. I don't want to be *special* to you, I want to be indispensable. A vital organ. Let me into your *heart,* Ethan. And while you've got the door open, let Sam and Linnet in, too."

"This *is* my heart!" he shouted. The words bounced off the pavement in the silence.

"What you've just offered is like the antechamber, all cleaned up and put on show for visitors. I want to be where the messy stuff happens."

He stared at her for a long moment, his breath coming quickly. "No one goes there," he said. "Not even me."

Cindy unlocked the car. "Then we don't have anything at all."

Cynthia woke next morning with the weight of the world on her chest and a bunch of new troubles knocking on her front door.

Literally. When her 7 a.m. visitor pounded harder, she knew for sure it couldn't be anything good.

Unless…unless it was Ethan, here to say he'd been a total jerk and he was wrong and he loved her and could she please come right into his heart and pull up a chair.

She hurried to the door, not caring that she was still in her pajamas. She was grinning as she flung the door open. "Hi!"

Linnet stumbled backward at the warmth of the welcome.

"Oh, uh, come in." Cynthia colored, but didn't explain herself. "I'll go find my robe."

When she returned to the kitchen, Linnet was pouring boiling water into the coffee press.

"Sorry to turn up so early," the older woman said. "I heard what happened to Sam."

"Everyone knows already?" Cynthia said, aghast. What was the bet they'd be lining up down the street for a seat in court today. Judge kisses Ethan, Ethan's son tries to burn down the community hall. She might as well stand up in court and announce to everyone that she and Ethan had broken up, just to cap it off.

"I don't think so," Linnet reassured her. "Ethan called me." Despite her worry, a wide smile stretched her mouth.

"He did?"

"Which is all thanks to you," Linnet continued. "Before you came along, I'd have been left to find out after the rest of the world. But he said—" her eyes shone "—he knows how important I am to Sam and that I want what's best for him." She added doubtfully, "He seems to think counseling will help Sam."

Cynthia grimaced. So much for the hope

that Ethan might have had an overnight epiphany.

"I have no idea where to begin with that boy, and I don't suppose he's forgiven me for reporting him for shoplifting," Linnet continued. "But if I can change, maybe Sam and Ethan can, too..." She stared down into her coffee.

"I hope you're right." Cynthia didn't want to disillusion her—Ethan would never change.

"You care about my son," Linnet said.

She nodded. "I can talk to him like I can to no one else."

Linnet paused, the milk carton in midair. "You find *Ethan* easy to talk to?"

"Well...yeah." Cynthia started to laugh. "I'm not saying it works the other way around."

"Just goes to show," Linnet said. "There's always hope."

Cynthia had asked Melanie to start work early, so they could be sure to be ready for Justice Pearson's visit. She was expecting him at nine o'clock, and had delayed the start of court until ten, so they'd have time to talk first.

She was as ready for him, from a professional perspective, as possible, she thought, as she aligned her computer keyboard with the edge of her desk. Although this wasn't a formal interview, she'd written down her ideas about judging—not that she would read them to him, but so she was sure they made sense and she had them clear in her own mind. She'd had the *Gazette* profile of her and the mayor and sheriff framed. Tania had mentioned the broom closet in her article, but it had been put in the context of Cynthia's rapid career elevation. Sympathetic.

"So, this hotshot justice is your boss?" Melanie asked as she ran a duster over the mantelpiece. Cynthia adjusted the robes she'd had cleaned after court yesterday, a rush job at Sparkle Linens.

"Not exactly. He's here to see how well I'm doing."

Melanie picked up Blind Justice, gave her a good wiping. "I always think this lady should take off her blindfold."

"The blindfold is the whole point," Cynthia said. "She's supposed to dispense justice based on the facts, without regard to race, color, creed and so on."

"But what about seeing people as people, not as part of a system?" Melanie asked.

"Sometimes you need to really look at people, see beyond the facts."

"That's true," Cynthia said slowly.

"Maybe she should just wear a patch over one eye," Melanie suggested.

Cynthia chortled. "Pirate Justice, a whole new form of law."

"I'm just saying..." Melanie set the figurine back on the mantel.

"Excuse me, ladies." Sheriff Davis had walked in without either of them noticing.

"The door didn't squeak," Cynthia said, surprised.

"I had the janitor oil it in honor of your guest today," Melanie told her.

"Thanks." She was touched by the woman's thoughtfulness. Except...now not only would people barge into her chambers, she wouldn't hear them coming. She realized the sheriff's expression was unusually somber. Her heart sank. "What's the problem, Sheriff?" *Please, don't let it be Sam.*

"Just had word from Judge Piet's son down Albany way," the sheriff said. "The judge passed away last night."

Melanie gave a cry of distress.

"I'm so sorry," Cynthia said. "From what I hear, everyone liked him."

"It was peaceful, not a bad way to go," the sheriff said. "You never met the guy, of course, but the news'll be all around town by lunchtime, so I thought I'd tell you myself."

"He'll be missed," Melanie said. "No offense to you, Judge Merritt. Now, that guest of yours is about to arrive, so I'd better get out to my desk to greet him properly."

Cynthia wondered if *she* would be missed when she left. And realized she would certainly miss Melanie.

Fifteen minutes later, Melanie stuck her head around the door. "Your guests are here, Judge Merritt."

"Bring the justice in please, Melanie." Hang on a minute...did she say *guests,* plural?

Had Justice Pearson brought another member of the selection committee along? Cynthia stood and straightened her jacket as Hal Pearson entered, followed by—

"Dad!" It came out a yelp, drawing a frown from Jonah as he entered her chambers. She hurried around the desk.

"Hello, Cynthia." He kissed her cheek, then patted her shoulder. "I thought I'd surprise you with a visit, my dear. I called Hal last night and asked if he had room in his car for me."

Assuming the justice drove some enormous Mercedes or similar, like most of his colleagues, space would never have been a problem. Cynthia shook hands with the justice, welcomed him warmly but professionally to her town.

My courthouse. Not my town.

And not her courthouse for much longer, if all went according to plan. With Judge Piet deceased, the town could appoint a permanent replacement. The timing couldn't be better for her to move on.

"So, Cynthia." Justice Pearson settled into the armchair she'd had Melanie bring in from the archive room. "Tell me how you've fared here in Stonewall Hollow?"

Cynthia glanced at her father. Surely he should leave? She was dismayed to find that her pleasure in seeing him had been diluted. He couldn't just love her and let her get on with the job in her own way?

"Don't worry about Jonah sitting in," the justice said. "This is very much an informal discussion. In fact, Jonah's presence makes it clear this isn't an interview. Since the selection process isn't formally underway, that's ideal."

"Great," she lied.

"Tell me everything," the justice said, "warts and all."

As if she was about to tell him she'd been public enemy number one for half her time here. Or that she'd taken on the most dangerous job in town and survived by the skin of her teeth. Or that she'd fallen in love with a taciturn rancher, the father of a local criminal.

"It's been an adjustment, getting into the small-town way of doing things." She explained about the personal stake everyone seemed to have in verdicts and sentencing.

"It may be an adjustment, but it seems to me you nailed it," her father said. "Hal and I hung around in the lobby downstairs for a few minutes, observing. A couple of people made comments about you."

Her stomach constricted, but she said calmly, "Oh, yes?"

"Positive comments," Hal clarified. "You command respect."

"I'm sure you'll find people who don't agree," she said fairly. Her dad looked worried, but Hal nodded approval.

"If everyone loved you, you wouldn't be doing your job," he said. "There's always someone with a grudge against the judge." He smirked at his own rhyme. "Can you walk me through a couple of the cases you've heard that have presented a particular challenge," he suggested, "and explain how you handled them?"

So much for his assertion this wasn't an interview. These were exactly the kinds of questions she'd expect if—when—she met the selection committee. Of course, if she didn't get the right answers now, she would never get as far as the committee.

"Hmm." She pretended to think, though they all knew she had some examples prepared. "Let me tell you about a contempt of court jailing."

She elaborated on the Paul Dayton story. Then, as she segued into another case, the door of her chambers burst open.

It was Ethan, unshaven, dark hair morning-shaggy, wearing jeans and a T-shirt that looked as if he'd slept in them. She was certain they were the ones he'd worn last night.

He didn't look as mad as he had last night, but there was a set determination in his face that boded ill.

"Cindy, I need to—" Ethan stopped and took stock of his surroundings. She had visitors, two men he'd never seen before, wearing suits that didn't look as if they'd been bought here in Stonewall Hollow.

He removed his hat. "Sorry, I didn't mean to interrupt."

Her expression was frozen; her gray eyes, usually clear to him, were unreadable. The guests stared at him as if he'd broken out of jail. Okay, he should have changed, and he shouldn't have barged in, but he'd been preoccupied with the need to tell Cindy he'd been an idiot last night. And, of course, preoccupied with Sam.

She was watching him, eyebrows lifted in the same way they had been the first day they'd met. Affection, no, something much stronger, rushed through him. "What do you plan to do with Sam's case today?"

Uh-oh. Totally the wrong thing to say. The jaw of one of her guests dropped; the other man appeared to want to see Ethan burn in hell. Who *were* they? Cindy drew herself up like a mare about to kick with lethal precision.

"Mr. Granger," she said, her voice arctic, "I have told you before, I will not entertain interference in my sentencing. If you wish to make a submission in court, talk to your son's lawyer."

Even that first day they'd met she hadn't been this cold. He remembered how he'd found her in the broom closet, how defensive she'd been. She was ten times more defensive now. He wanted to haul her into his arms and tell her it would be okay and he wouldn't let anyone hurt her.

"I shouldn't have said that," he apologized. "But I was thinking about what you said last night—" one of her guests was turning purple "—and maybe I need to make some changes."

Just like that, the atmosphere shifted. The hostility thawed in Cindy and she relaxed.

"You have guests," he said belatedly, "so I won't go into it now. I'll call you later."

He rammed his hat back on his head.

"Ethan," she said.

His own name had never been so welcome. He spun back to her.

"I'd like—" she drew a breath "—to introduce you to my father, Jonah Merritt." The guy with the purple face.

Hell. Jonah Merritt stood. He was tall—not as tall as Ethan but his solid build conveyed power. No sign of the ill health Cindy said he'd suffered. Jonah shook Ethan's hand warily.

"And this is Justice Hal Pearson from Atlanta," Cindy said.

For the first time, Ethan took a proper look at the other man. His insides froze. He thanked God for the years of self-discipline, of hiding his emotions. He shook the justice's hand calmly. And quickly turned back to Jonah.

"Welcome to Stonewall Hollow, sir," he said. "I've heard a lot about you."

Cindy winced. "Ethan runs a program for young offenders on his ranch. He's achieved quite remarkable reductions in recidivism." Her father didn't look impressed. "He has a degree in criminal justice," she added.

Don't tell him that, it'll all start adding up. Ethan closed his eyes. Could this get any worse?

"Where did you go to school?" Jonah asked.

"I got my degree from Ohio University." Instinct warned him to tell the truth, the whole truth and nothing but the truth *right now.* But how could he tell Cindy what he should have told her weeks ago in front of her dad and a guy who likely had something to do with that promotion she wanted?

He kept his face averted from Justice Pearson. Jonah said, "Cynthia, this man's interruption is the sort of thing you meant by people overstepping the boundaries." He jerked his head at Ethan.

She'd complained about him to her dad? Not about him, he realized, about the whole town in those early days.

"It's a matter of understanding the local psyche and respecting that not everyone does things the city way," she said. "As long as the law continues to frame the process and the outcome." She carried on talking jargon Ethan could have understood if he'd bothered to try. He was too busy understanding Cindy's relationship with her dad. She was obviously out to please him at any cost. Last night she'd said she knew how it felt to worry that her father didn't love her, that his feelings were tied up in how good she was at her job, not in that she was his daughter.

She deserved better. He wanted to punch Jonah for making her feel less than loved… then maybe he should punch himself while he was at it.

Now wasn't the time to tackle her dad, but if he was going to dole out affection based on achievement, Ethan would help her get her fair share. "It's fair to say, sir, that Cindy, uh,

Cynthia, has earned the respect of the whole town. Which wasn't easy."

This time she looked at him with warmth and gratitude. "Her legal integrity is beyond question," he said, "even if folk don't always like the verdict, they haven't been able to point to any irregularity or inconsistency."

Jonah was nodding, but enough suspicion remained to tell Ethan the man had guessed that his relationship with Cindy overstepped the professional boundary.

This was way more than Ethan had bargained for when he came out this morning. But as some small compensation, there was definite approval in Jonah's eyes as he regarded his daughter.

Then Justice Pearson said, "Do I know you, sir?"

Uh-oh.

"I *do* know you." The justice's eyes narrowed. "It must have been some years ago, but I have an excellent memory for faces..."

Great, couldn't Ethan have had a judge who had a terrible memory for faces?

"You were in my courtroom," Justice Pearson said triumphantly. "Up for aggravated assault."

Chapter Sixteen

Ethan hooked his thumbs in his pockets. His eyes found Cynthia's as he replied to Justice Pearson. "You sentenced me to ten years. I served five."

The office dissolved around her, people and objects swimming through her vision. Ethan had served time. In jail. For assault. Five years.

"That's where you did your degree," she said, the revelation as painful as it was obvious. "In prison."

He nodded. "Distance learning in Ohio University's College Program for the Incarcerated."

She shuddered convulsively. "Your work scheme on the ranch…"

"Is intended to get through to kids before they end up like I did, too angry to control themselves."

No wonder he was afraid of losing his temper! No wonder Sam's mother had decided her son was better off not having his father.

"I should have told you, Cindy," he said. "I wanted to. I'm sorry. But no one around here knows, apart from my mom. She and I agreed to put it behind us."

"You haven't even told Sam?" she said, aghast.

She put her hand to her mouth; this had to stop. She couldn't have this conversation in front of her dad and Harold. She looked like a total fool…exactly what she was. Ethan was a convicted criminal! He'd kissed her, seduced her…made her fall in love with him…aware that if she'd had full possession of the facts she would never…

Her instinct was to usher everyone out of her chambers, then dive into the broom closet. Curl up in a ball with her hands over her head until the pain went away.

What would her dad be thinking? All her

objections to his emotional manipulation melted away. He was all she had.

"Cynthia." Her father was studying her, attempting to read her mind. "You and this—this man, you're not..."

She didn't let him finish. "When I first arrived here I had some questions about Ethan's rehabilitation program. That's caused some friction. I see now why he didn't want me inquiring too closely into his work."

"Hey," Ethan protested. She shot him a killing look. It left him distressingly still alive. "Think what you like of my past," he said, "but don't diss the work I do with those kids."

She would do whatever she had to. She'd lost any hope of a relationship with Ethan—which had only ever been a false hope, she saw now. Hadn't she told him she wanted an *honest* relationship? And he'd kept this from her. She wasn't about to lose her new job, her father's respect...everything.

Nor was she about to get in the broom closet. She would do her best to win her father back, but if she failed, she wasn't going to collapse.

She wanted to order Ethan out of her chambers, but she couldn't afford to have him refuse to leave.

"As I said to you a while back, Dad," she continued, "conflict of interest is a real problem here." She widened her focus to include Justice Pearson, shooting him a confident smile. "It's fair to say small town is a synonym for conflict of interest." Both her father and the justice chuckled, albeit warily, at the phrase she'd stolen from Ethan.

"There's a further problem," she said, "in that people are unrealistic about the role of a judge—it's a fundamental lack of understanding of the judicial hierarchy. I ended up judging cakes and cookies at the county fair." Hal laughed at the ludicrousness of it.

Cynthia pushed aside the thought that it had been one of the most satisfying days of her life. "I'm also expected to boost storekeepers' morale by clamping down on shoplifting, to consider DUI defendants' transportation problems, and to…" She spread her hands. "Well, it's been a challenge, to say the least."

Hal was looking at her with exactly the right blend of sympathy and admiration. Approval gleamed in her dad's eyes.

"That's not what you think of us," Ethan said harshly. "You don't just think we're a bunch of hicks who don't understand how the law works."

"Careful," Hal said.

"I'm not in your court now, *Justice,*" Ethan retorted. "This is my town, my home. A place I love. A place I thought Cindy was growing to love." His eyes bored into her, but he was the one who was out of line here, not her. She lifted her chin and looked down her nose at him.

"You might just be talking to the next member of Georgia's superior court bench," Justice Pearson warned. Jonah practically punched the air in excitement. "Then next time you're up on an assault charge…"

"I'm not the man I was then." Ethan's gaze flickered to Cynthia, as if he'd realized he was repeating what she'd said to him.

He ran a hand through his hair, making it stand up and look even messier.

"Cindy," he said, "I should have told you."

"But you wouldn't," she said. "You never do, Ethan."

"Dammit, Cindy, listen to me!"

"Sadly," Jonah said to the justice, "our prison system leaves some people with a resentment for authority that they never shake off."

The justice nodded. "While others are just

trouble from the moment they step into the dock, and you know they always will be."

"Oh, for f—" Ethan stopped.

Cynthia should be glad that his refusal to lose his temper wouldn't let him say the things that would offend Justice Pearson. Otherwise she would be tainted by association and would lose any chance of getting this job. Already, she felt sick at the thought of explaining all this to her father, trying to restore his faith in her.

Real love isn't about what someone does or doesn't do. It's about who they are in your life. If that was true, she wouldn't have to work so hard with her dad… She quashed the thought—taking relationship advice from Ethan was like asking a tobacconist how to quit smoking.

"Cindy," Ethan said, "let's finish that conversation we started last night. Tell me how you feel." What, he expected her to bare her feelings in front of the justice and her father, while he got to keep his locked away?

"You agreed with me that love should be about who people are to you, not about what they've done," Ethan said. "Where's that, now you know I have a criminal record? Or does that only apply to your father?"

She sensed Jonah's mounting alarm. "You've held up our meeting long enough," she said. "Goodbye, Ethan."

He drew in a sharp breath. Then he headed for the door. "See you around, Judge."

"See you in court," she snapped back, the hurt of his deception still knifing her. She'd thought Ethan was opening up, in his own limited way, and all along he'd kept his past from her. She'd been crazy to even contemplate making a place for herself here in Stonewall Hollow. To dare to hope she had a place in Ethan's heart.

She turned back to the justice, schooling her expression. "I'm sorry you had to witness that, Hal, Dad. As I said, this job isn't always easy."

"You handled that hothead well," Hal said.

"Thank you, but I have to admit I'm feeling I made a mistake," she said calmly. "When I first felt doubts about Ethan's program I should have inquired more deeply into his background. Instead, I accepted the recommendations of the sheriff and the probation officer."

"I appreciate your willingness to be held accountable," Hal said. "Everyone makes mistakes, Cynthia. It's whether you learn from them or not that sets the winners apart from the losers."

"You're right," she murmured. Ethan had learned from his mistakes, the bad youth had become a good man...but he hadn't quite learned enough.

"I think we've covered the essentials." Hal stood. Her dad did the same. The justice shook her hand warmly. "You'll need time to prepare yourself mentally for court, I know I always do. We'll see you in there."

"Of course." She turned to her father. "Dad, I want to come back to Atlanta."

"I don't think—"

"I've learned everything I can here," she said. "Whether or not I'm honored enough to be appointed to the superior court, I'm coming home." She'd never been so firm with him. She eyed him without blinking.

"Of course you should come home," he said. "We all miss you."

Cynthia nodded, but didn't let her relief show. She would be gone, soon, and Ethan couldn't hurt her.

"All rise for the Honorable Judge Merritt presiding," the bailiff announced.

Cynthia walked to the bench, careful not

to focus on the public seating in case she saw Ethan. As the morning's work got underway, she settled into the rhythm of listening, questioning, listening some more, judging. A wave of calm carried her along, giving her a clarity of vision that was almost painful.

A DUI, neighbors disputing a fence line, a simple assault—she dispatched each case efficiently and without conflict. One of the defendants even thanked her for her sentence.

The last ticket on the morning's docket was Sam Barrett, with criminal trespass added to the shoplifting charge. He stepped up into the dock appearing far more subdued than he had the first time. She saw his mute appeal, fear. Under the law he was an adult...but right now he seemed more like a confused, unhappy child. Tom Cadman, the lawyer, looked at her expectantly. She was supposed to order a transfer to the court in Gonville.

Where the sentencing judge would take one glance at Sam's escalating record and see a young man headed for major trouble. He might throw him into jail as a warning.

It might work, but Cynthia didn't believe Sam got into trouble for any reason other than to force Ethan to show some emotion. In which case, jail wouldn't do a thing for him. Other than screw him up the way his father had been screwed up.

Blind Justice. She thought about what Melanie had said earlier, about seeing beyond the law at the people involved. A legal system couldn't work like that, of course, it needed structure and rules. But did that have to preclude compassion, good sense?

Cynthia thought about what Ethan had said in her chambers this morning. Not the I'm-a-convicted-felon part, but that brief acknowledgment he needed to make some changes. She wondered if he meant it, if he could change enough to save Sam.

She cleared her throat. "How does the defendant plead?"

She was telling the lawyer, and Ethan and Sam, that she would hear this case. If they thought she was too personally involved, they could appeal later. But now she was going to do her best for Ethan. And Sam.

Sam pleaded guilty. As Ethan said, he was honest, which gave her reason to hope. The D.A. presented his case, then Sam's lawyer did his best to show that Sam was a good kid at heart. A challenge that was getting tougher with each new charge.

Eventually, it was time to pronounce her

judgment. She could defer sentencing to another day, so she didn't have to do this in front of her father and Justice Pearson. But who knew how soon she would leave. And Sam needed help now.

"Mr. Ethan Granger has some recommendations for sentencing," Sam's lawyer announced.

Ethan stood slowly, almost painfully. Sam's eyes sought his father's but Ethan was focused on the bench. On her.

Don't blow it. Give me something to work with. Give Sam some hope.

"Your Honor," Ethan began. It was difficult to look at Cindy when he'd just hurt her so badly...and when she'd hurt him. But he couldn't take his eyes off her. Couldn't unscramble his brain to give the argument he'd prepared. It was all getting mixed up with the words she'd thrown at him last night.

"I want to ask the Court..." He paused, glanced at Sam. His son's glazed expression said he was a thousand miles away and right this moment thumbing a lift out of Ethan's life, out of his heart. He'd never make it, of course, Ethan would never let Sam out of his heart.

"Mr. Granger," Cindy said, and he realized the silence had grown to elephantine proportions.

He cleared his throat. "As I was saying..."

She leaned forward over the bench and said, slowly, deliberately, "Say something else." Her voice was low and urgent.

"Excuse me?" He stared at her.

He saw a hint of a smile on that mouth that drove him wild in so many ways—kissing him, telling him how to raise his son, accusing him of all kinds of things. Saying she thought about forever when she was with him. "Mr. Granger, how did you feel when you heard Sam had been arrested for vandalism?" The question she'd asked that very first day in court.

"I was disappointed," he said, as he'd said then.

She didn't reply, just sat back, her hands folded in front of her.

Sam's eyes lasered into him, twin points of burning heat. What had Cindy said, that the boy didn't know Ethan loved him? Garbage. Of course he did. Ethan might not have said those words, but Sam had seen his love in the way he stood beside him when he was in trouble. In his eagerness to have Sam with him at the ranch for his community service. In the way he controlled his temper when Sam did his best to provoke him. The way he hadn't thrown him out.

Exactly the same things he did for every other kid in trouble in this town.

The realization hit Ethan like a runaway freight train. *Hell.* Cindy was right. Sam didn't have the faintest clue.

She was watching him now. As if she anticipated what he had to say, but didn't believe he'd do it. Sam's expression mirrored hers, Ethan noticed, but without the smidgen of hope.

"I was angry," Ethan said quietly. "Sam is my son—" his voice grew in strength "—and although I haven't been in his life very long—and I'll regret to the end of my days that I wasn't there for him when he was younger—I love him like there's no tomorrow."

Sam's mouth dropped open; so did Cindy's. Ethan almost laughed. But he was fighting for his life here.

"Sam's mom threw him out of his home because of the trouble he was getting into, and I know from experience that kind of rejection is about the toughest thing that can happen to a kid." Linnet was in the front row, but he figured she would understand he needed to say this. "When he got here, instead of finding what he needed—a dad who understood him and would reassure him he was loved—he found me. A jerk with a ton of good intentions, but no clue how to say something as simple as *I love you*. Sam, you're my son, I love you, but I have to tell you, you ever screw up like this again, I'll kill you."

Sam gulped; he blinked rapidly. But he didn't make eye contact with Ethan. What had Ethan expected? That Sam would say, "I love you, too, Dad," and they'd have a Hallmark moment right there in court? As if anything worth having had ever come that easy.

"Your Honor," Ethan said to Cindy, "I'm not going to kill Sam, I love him. But this trouble he's in is killing both of us. I'm asking you to give me and my son a chance." He could have stood right here and announced he loved her, too—that was what he'd realized overnight though the full impact hadn't hit him yet. But there was no chance for him and her. Even if he opened his heart, this morning had changed things. She knew his past, which would surely be insurmountable for a superior court judge.

Cindy was staring down at her notes. The

silence in the courtroom was complete, he could have heard an onion growing.

At last, she lifted her head. "Samuel Barrett, you have pleaded guilty to criminal trespass." As her clear voice rang through the courtroom, Ethan saw Sam's shame. "Unlike some of the young people who appear before me," she continued, "you don't have to face the consequences of your actions alone. You have a father who loves you more than he loves his own life—" Ethan's gaze flew to hers, she wasn't prone to using such emotional words in court "—and a loving grandmother. You are, in fact, lucky. And today—" she half smiled "—is your lucky day. I sentence you to work with your father, to talk to him every day for however long it takes for you two stubborn idiots to realize how much you mean to each other."

Sam half laughed, half sobbed. Ethan knuckled his eyes. He caught a flash of horror on the face of Bert Gregg, one of the town's toughest men. Bert would never be caught close to tears over Bert Jr. But Bert's wife, Hazel, gave Ethan a tender look. Several other women did the same.

"When you believe you have reached that

stage," Cindy continued, "you may apply to the court for discharge of your sentence."

She would be gone by then.

"Thank you, Your Honor," Sam said. She smiled at him.

"Mr. Granger." Her voice was frosty, with none of the compassion she'd directed at Sam.

"Yes, Your Honor?"

She leaned forward and her eyes narrowed. "Don't blow it."

On Monday, someone from the Justice Department called Cynthia and told her this was her last week in Stonewall Hollow. An interim judge had been found to replace her. She called her father, only to find he'd heard already.

When she told Melanie, her assistant's eyes swam in a pool of tears. "Cynthia, honey, I'm gonna miss you." They hugged.

"I'll miss you, too," Cynthia said honestly.

When Melanie left, she got back to her paperwork. But she found herself, yet again, rereading the document she kept hidden in her briefcase. The transcript of Ethan's trial from sixteen years ago. She'd ordered a copy from the state court in Atlanta.

She didn't need the pages—she'd memorized the most important parts. Ethan had found a minimum-wage job in a café in Atlanta, a place he'd eaten with his mom and his stepfather a few times over the years. His stepfather, Wayne, discovered Ethan working there, and took to lunching there when he was in town. Mainly so he could taunt and provoke Ethan with stories about how much happier his mom was now that Ethan was gone.

One day, Ethan snapped. He lashed out at Wayne, punching him. As his stepfather went down, his head struck the corner of a table. What turned the fracas from simple assault—a misdemeanor—to aggravated assault was Ethan's yelled "I'll kill you." The D.A. took one look at Ethan's record of misdemeanors and decided he was a danger to society. Justice Pearson had agreed that Ethan had "intent to murder" and jailed him.

Cynthia had wept the first time she'd read about the man she loved, then only eighteen years old, being manipulated by his sick stepfather. It reminded her of Ethan's comment the day they met that justice wasn't always served by the law.

At lunchtime, the door to Cynthia's chambers was pushed open, and a delegation entered without knocking. The mayor, the sheriff, Jackson Bream and Mrs. Baker.

"A moment of your time, Judge," the mayor said.

"Of course." Cynthia didn't have enough chairs for them all to sit, so she stood out of courtesy.

"We've come to ask you to consider staying on as Stonewall Hollow's judge," Jackson Bream said.

"Really?" It was the last thing she'd expected. "But...why?"

"You understand this town," Mrs. Baker said. "You have guts."

"You do a good job, Judge," the sheriff said, dispassionate as ever. She'd taken that for coolness when they'd first met. Now she knew better.

"And we like you," the mayor said. "Most everyone does. Maybe not Tania from the *Gazette,* or Paul Dayton, but the rest of us do."

We like you. Simple words that meant so much. Cynthia's laugh came out shaky. "I'm honored, truly honored." And she was. To be chosen because people liked her and because she fit in was more precious than any trial victory. She was almost tempted to accept.

Almost. "But my family is in Atlanta, and right now, I need to be with them."

"Ah, you're upset about breaking up with Ethan," Mrs. Baker said sagely.

Cynthia laughed out loud. Why not just shout it from the rooftops?

Chapter Seventeen

Cindy had been gone two weeks, and Ethan missed her so much it hurt. Things were going better at home—he and Linnet were making an effort, and Sam had calmed down. But nothing was quite right.

It was no use telling her she couldn't get access to his heart. She was already there, opening the place up, airing it to the world. She'd been in town a month, one lousy month, but she'd burrowed so deep it was as if she'd always been there and always would be.

There had to be something he could do, he just didn't know what.

But it involved telling her he loved her.

And he'd figured out how to do it, too. He didn't have a great track record with saying the words, and his troubles with Sam proved he wasn't as good as he'd like to be at showing it, but there was one more way.

"Dad?" Sam said.

"What?" Ethan had spoken too sharply. "Sorry, son, I was miles away." In Atlanta, with Cindy. Where his brain spent most of its time these days.

"No kidding." But Sam's rejoinder didn't come out the way it would have a few weeks ago, wrapped in attitude.

"What's the problem?" Ethan went to where Sam was attaching a fence wire to its post—a quick Sunday afternoon job.

"This damn thing won't friggin' reach." They were working on Sam's cussing. Ethan decided to be grateful for the *friggin'*, milder than Sam's usual choice, and let the *damn* slide. A man had to pick his battles.

"Let's take a look." Ethan reveled in his closeness to Sam. The whiff of teenage boy was powerful on a hot day like this, but he loved it.

Together they pulled the wire taut. Sam hammered in a staple to hold it in place.

They got back to the house as Linnet arrived. She'd dressed up for the occasion in a frilly pink blouse and deeper pink skirt.

"Happy birthday, Ethan." She kissed his cheek, then handed over a small rectangular package.

"Thanks, Mom. I'll open it inside." He took the casserole dish she got out of the car. "What's for dinner?"

"I made chili," Linnet said. It had been his favorite as a kid. They were trying, all of them.

"Great." In the kitchen, he set the casserole down on the counter, then moved to the dining table to open his present.

"I didn't get you anything," Sam warned. "I'm still paying off my court fines."

"Pleased to hear it. That thing on the wall is enough for me." *That thing* was a commendation for bravery awarded to Sam for saving the little boy at the rodeo. Ethan grinned at his son, unable to hide his pride, then he tore off the silver paper, aware of Linnet's fidgeting. It was a pen, chunky, brushed steel that would sit comfortably in a man's hand. He laughed. "Are you psychic, Mom?"

"Why?" she said anxiously.

He leaned across and kissed her cheek. "I've decided to take up letter-writing."

"Really?" she said, pleased.

"Yep. In fact, I've written a couple already. Sam, if you look in that drawer in the desk where I keep all the bills, you'll find them."

Curiosity had Sam obeying. He returned from the den holding two envelopes. "There's one for you, Gram, and one for me." He gave Ethan a nervous grin.

"What's this about?" Linnet asked.

"Kind of a birthday present from me to you," Ethan said. "Open them while I put the chili on to heat."

He washed his hands and began to putter in the kitchen. No noise from the dining table, other than the rustle of paper.

He forced himself to relax as he turned on the gas burner and gave the chili a stir. He'd done what Cindy wanted—opened his heart and told his son and his mother his deepest feelings. Not out loud, because he wasn't that kind of guy. But on paper, he'd said everything they needed to hear.

I was a brat, Mom, and then a jerk, he'd said in Linnet's letter.

Yes, Wayne was a jerk, too, but with him making your life miserable there was no need for me to do the same. I don't blame

> you for throwing me out. I hated you for it for a long time, but I don't anymore. You're my mom, I love and respect you, and I don't ever want anything to come between us again.

He glanced at his mom, saw tears sliding down her cheeks. She looked up, saw him, smiled. A tender smile. Then she bent to the letter again.

He heard a smothered sound from Sam—probably he was up to the part where Ethan told him about his time in prison. About the kind of guy he'd been.

I'm sorry, Sam, he'd written toward the end of the letter.

> Sorry I was such a loser your mother couldn't tell you about me, couldn't tell me I had a son. Sorry I missed those early years of your life, and when I did get to know you, I screwed up. Most of all, I'm sorry it took you trying to start a fire and Cindy hauling me up in court for me to tell you to your face that I love you. Well, you know now, and I'll make sure I say it more often. Or maybe I'll write it—seems easier somehow. But

please trust that no matter what happens, no matter what you do, you're my son and I'll always treasure you and love you."

"Friggin' hell, Dad." Tears streaked Sam's cheeks, too. He wiped them away irritably. "Did you have to say all this freakin' stuff?"

Ethan walked over to the table, slung an arm around his son's shoulder, pressed what would probably be his first and last kiss to Sam's hair. "My son, practically a PG-cusser," he said proudly.

And they were all laughing.

It wasn't until they sat down to eat that Linnet asked the question. "So, Sam," she said slyly, "were there any other letters in that desk drawer?"

Sam grinned. "Matter of fact, there was one. To Cindy."

"Ah," Linnet said.

"I'll say the blessing." Ethan bowed his head and prayed, which shut them up.

Not for long.

"Why haven't you sent Cindy her letter?" Linnet asked as she spread her napkin on her lap.

"I'm not sure I've got it right," he admitted. Cindy's had been both the hardest and the easiest letter. Easiest because they didn't have a huge history to get over. Hardest because he was scared he'd screw up and he wouldn't get another chance. Hell, he wasn't sure he had any chance at all.

Sam spoke up. "Cindy came to see me the day I...you know."

"The day you tried to set fire to the hall," Ethan said firmly. "We have a new policy around here, folks, nothing gets swept under the table. We acknowledge what happened, then we move on."

"Whatever." Sam rolled his eyes. "Cindy told me a lot of stuff about you—the kind of stuff that was in your letter." Sam blushed to his ears. "I couldn't handle it, man, what the hell was I meant to do?"

"We are all aware what you decided on," Linnet said tartly, buying into the new openness.

"I went to see Jacko and the other guys," Sam said. Jacko Wallace, aka Trouble. "I kind of told them what Cindy said."

"I'll bet they had some good advice." Ethan didn't hold back the sarcasm.

"They reckoned you and her were, like, messing with my head. That's why I decided to start the fire—I wanted to prove you couldn't manipulate me."

Ethan thumped his hand down on the table. "For crying out loud, that's the stupidest thing I ever heard. If Jacko Wallace told you to set fire to your hair would you do that?"

Sam reddened. "Shut up, Dad, you sound crazy."

"You *are* crazy," he snapped. "A certified nut job."

They glared at each other, bristling like two hedgehogs, until Linnet said mildly, "Boys, boys."

They turned to her.

"You don't have time for this argument, Ethan. Cindy told me she always has dinner at her dad's place on Sunday nights."

"I'm not sure Cindy's ready to be a step-mom." He said it for Sam's sake.

"Dad, I already have a mother." Sam looked down at his place mat, then at the phone on the wall. "I guess I should call her."

"Great idea," Ethan said. "Now's good."

"I'll do it later," Sam said. Before Ethan could argue, he added, "After you leave for Atlanta."

There was one other reason Ethan was hesitating to give Cindy the letter. In it, he'd said everything he felt. Put himself on the line, no going back.

Could he give Cindy his whole heart?

I already have.

Could he convince her to accept it?

Ethan pushed his chili away. “You’re right, Mom.”

It seemed it was destined to be a night of firsts.

Chapter Eighteen

The doorbell rang as Sabrina poured the coffee. Jonah put down the glass of red wine he insisted was good for his heart. "Are we expecting anyone?"

"I'll get it." Megan left the room.

They were still at the dining table, with the windows open—it was a muggy night. Cynthia glanced at her watch and wondered how soon she could excuse herself. Nine o'clock. Not yet.

"Cynthia, sweetheart, did you get enough to eat?" her father asked.

"I'm fine, Dad."

He'd been worried about her since she returned from Stonewall Hollow. She'd accepted the offer of an interview for the judgeship, but she'd told Jonah she wasn't certain she wanted the job. He'd immediately assumed she was still suffering from stress, and was being solicitous toward her in a way he'd always been with Sabrina, seldom with her. She allowed herself to enjoy it, rather than see it as a sign of weakness in herself.

She wasn't going to rush into anything. She loved the law, she couldn't envisage any other career, but maybe she didn't want to be a superior court judge.

Megan sashayed back into the room. "Someone to see you, *Cindy.*"

Cynthia looked up as her sister stepped aside.

"Ethan!"

He looked incredible in jeans and a black shirt, open at the neck, his hat in his hand. Her love for him surged, undiminished.

"You!" Jonah thundered.

Ethan gave him a patient nod. "Mr. Merritt, everyone, I'm sorry to interrupt your evening, but I need to talk to Cindy."

Jonah balled his napkin and threw it down. Hands on the table, he levered himself to his feet.

"Would you like coffee, Ethan?" Sabrina asked unfazed, the perfect hostess. "Jake, darling, could you go bring another cup?"

Ethan grinned at her. "Maybe later, thanks." He walked around the table.

Questions streamed through Cynthia's mind. He'd come for her, of course—the smile in his eyes told her that. But what was he offering?

When he reached her, he held out a hand. She stared at it. She'd missed him so much, she didn't want to hope.

"Come back to me, Cindy."

"Now look here," Jonah began.

"I love you. I should have said it weeks ago, but I was an idiot. But since you've been gone—hell, Cindy, without you I don't fit in my own skin."

Sabrina sighed.

Skin. A vital organ. Cynthia put her hand in his, let him draw her to her feet.

"Cynthia," her dad said sharply, "the man is a felon."

Indrawn breaths around the table. *Thanks, Dad.*

"Wrong," Ethan said. "I *used* to be a felon. Life gave me a second chance, and now I'm hoping Cindy will do the same."

Megan's face was a study in mixed emotions.

"My daughter has an exceptional career in the judiciary," Jonah said. "If you really love her..."

"Dad," Cynthia protested. "Be quiet."

Her father gaped.

"Does this place have a broom closet?" Ethan asked.

"By the front door," she said.

"Let's go."

He led her from the room. As she passed Sabrina, Sabrina murmured, "Way to go, Cyn."

When they reached the broom closet, Ethan opened the door and pulled her inside.

"What are you doing?" Her dad would have her certified.

He turned on the light. "Wow, this is the Ritz of broom closets—it's enormous. We could live in here." He closed the door.

She giggled, her heart growing lighter by the second. "I'm borderline crazy, remember? Don't encourage me."

"Oh, I intend to encourage you. I plan to encourage you to be anything you want, as long as it involves spending your life with me."

She grabbed his hands. "I want that, but I

can't be with a man who can't figure out his feelings and make them plain."

"Weren't you listening out there? I love you, Cindy, to the bottom of my heart."

He wrapped his arms around her and lowered his mouth to hers. She'd missed this, wanted this, hungered for it. She kissed him back, until they both shook with desire.

"Marry me," he said.

"Yes." Then she thumped him. "No!"

He laughed. "Why doesn't this surprise me?"

"You make it sound simple, but you've got a lot to sort out. What makes you think you can handle the kind of all-encompassing relationship I want?"

Ethan sighed. "Let's sit down, this might take a while." He nudged a bucket aside with his foot. A broom clattered to the floor.

"Cynthia, are you all right?" Her father was outside the closet.

"I'm fine, Dad, I'll be out in a minute."

They waited. A minute later, Cynthia heard the murmur of Sabrina's voice, then two sets of fading footsteps.

Ethan sat on the floor, his back to the wall. Cynthia sat between his legs, her back to his chest. His hands caressed her waist, her thighs. It wasn't enough; she twisted to reach his mouth, then she ended up facing him, kneeling between his legs.

"Kissing in a broom closet." Ethan sounded dazed when he surfaced. "Can't think why I never tried it before." He nuzzled her neck. "Have you ever made love in one of these?"

She stifled a shriek of laughter.

"I'm serious." He reached for the zipper of her dress.

She slapped his hands away. "Talk first, before you get your hands on me." As if she was about to make love with him in her dad's broom closet. But she didn't want to discourage him, so she held off on mentioning that. She tucked her hair behind her ears. "Tell me more about this loving me from the bottom of your heart."

"Here." He fumbled in his trouser pocket and pulled out an envelope. "You can read all about it."

She examined the envelope. "You wrote me a letter?"

"Every last, sappy feeling in black and white," he confirmed. "I wrote letters to Sam and Mom, too, but yours is the only one that's X-rated."

She felt herself blush. "How are things with Sam?"

"Great, or getting there. We're not bosom buddies yet—the only bosom I really want to get close to is yours." He peered down the deep V of her dress.

"What's with your sudden passion for letter-writing?"

"It turns out I can write my feelings down better than I can talk about them."

"Amazing." She started to open the envelope.

He covered her hand with his. "Cindy, I know I'm not the guy you imagined ending up with."

Thank goodness.

"And if my prison record is going to stop you getting that job, then maybe we need to wait until you've got the job before we—"

"Aren't they still looking for a judge in Stonewall Hollow?" she interrupted.

"Well, yeah, but you don't want…do you?" A slow smile broke over his face.

"Hey, these are the first people who ever liked me," she said. "That's a powerful draw."

"Everyone likes you," he chided her.

"Well, there's a certain pigheaded, sexy

rancher whose opinion matters more than most…" She kissed him.

Ethan growled low in his throat. "I haven't finished telling you how I feel. I've got so many lyrical words waiting to get out."

She laughed. "Save them, we have the rest of our lives."

He grabbed her by the arms. "Does this mean you'll marry me?"

"Oh, yeah."

Their kisses turned combustible.

"I want a closet like this in our home," he said raggedly. "I'll build one."

"Great idea," she panted. She moved around to sit next to him, back to the wall. "Did I mention there are two conditions to my coming back to Stonewall Hollow?"

"Name them," he said. "I'll do whatever it takes. Even if I have to bare my heart to you every damn day."

"Mmm, that's good," she said. "Three conditions, then."

He swatted her. "What are the other two?"

"One, I never have to judge a cake contest again."

"Done. I'll tell Jackson the good news. What else?"

"I want a lock on my chambers door."

"I'll fit it myself," he said. "When you and I are making love in that broom closet, we don't want anyone walking in on us."

She kissed his chin.

"Okay, Your Honor." He put up his hand, as if he was swearing an oath. "Are you ready to make an honest man of me?"

"You've made a very compelling case, Mr. Granger," she said. "I sentence you to a lifetime of marriage to me."

"Whatever you say, Your Honor," he murmured, before his mouth covered hers.

* * * * *